SECRET OF CERES BOOK 2

DAUNTLESS

STELLA WILLIAMS

Editied by Raw Book Editing www.rawbookediting.com
Book Cover Design by RebeccaCovers

First Edition: February 2020
ISBN: 978-1-7335638-9-5

Published by

Serpentine Creative LLC
www.serpentinecreative.com

For all the women who exemplify Black Girl Magic.

Prologue

Tick. Tick. Tick. For a moment, Renata's subconscious took her to the small apartment of her nightmares. The only memory of her life before the orphanage. Two bedrooms, barely furnished, but full of people. Laying on the couch, on the floor. Peaceful and unmoving as Renata crawled by. The only movement the swinging pendulum of a large grandfather clock.

Tick, Tick, Tick.

She crawled to the window, desperate for air. Tiny hands struggled to push the window to the fire escape open.

"No! Don't!" Her adult brain cried out to her toddler self as if she could change what happened.

The window finally budged, the first rush of cool air a welcome relief before the end. Gasping for air, Renata's eyes flew open. Sweat dripped into her eyes, delaying her realization that they were covered. Disoriented, she had no idea where she was. Her head felt fuzzy like static on the radio.

Am I still dreaming?

A chill ran up her spine as her senses slowly came back to her. She was still locked in a nightmare, a living nightmare.

Tick. Tick. Tick.

Strips of thick fabric bound her wrists and ankles. Luxurious fabric that felt velvety and soft. The opposite of what one would assume to be used by kidnappers. Yet, no amount of twisting or straining loosened their hold. Renata refused to give up despite being unable to move more than her head.

Tick, Tick, Tick.

Renata couldn't be sure if the sound was real or a figment of her imagination. The only sound she could make out in the silence. The marking of time; she'd cheated death once, and now it was back to claim her. Using her one memory of where she came from to torture her in her final moments. She counted to keep from going insane.

Six hundred seven, six hundred eight, six hundred nine.

There was a moan to her left, and she lost track of her count. She turned her head toward the sound. She couldn't see through the blindfold over her eyes, but apparently, she wasn't alone after all. She was just the first to wake. Shifting and muffled shrieking from her unknown companion let her know the person beside her was in the same predicament.

Please, God! Any God! Let me get out of this alive!

Her silent prayer for salvation had yet to be answered. If only Renata had listened to the young girl in the first location. The frazzled young girl who tried to warn her about the danger she faced.

Renata hadn't wanted to listen then. Too afraid, too arrogant, and too stupid to heed the warning not to use her energy abilities to escape. Now, as what Renata could only assume was death lurked around every corner. How could she not feel like this was somehow her fault? She should never have gone to Club Obelisk. It was a risk as it was rumored to be a Vampire hangout, and there was a serial killer on the prowl. Renata had been tired of hiding out, tired of running, and tired of hiding her true self.

Sure, she could have gone to a Resistance meeting instead, but she wasn't quite ready to buy into the entire rebellionchilada they had going. Not to mention, she'd already barked up the Jaq Andromeda tree and didn't want to admit she took his passing interest a little too seriously.

Something that now seemed so trivial had led to her decision to head to Club Obelisk instead. At the time, it seemed the perfect place to let loose. Just once in her life—only Renata had gotten a little too loose. She'd let her guard down, overestimating her ability to read the human male's energy. She'd sensed the darkness in him, but that wasn't unusual for humans who preferred the company of Vampires to that of their own kind.

Stupid, stupid, stupid!

If Renata could have kicked her own butt with her restraints she would have. Thinking back on how everything had gone down, it had to be the drink he'd bought her. Her order of a vodka cranberry had tasted a little on the sweet side. After a few sips, she was waking up at the first location. A basement room with two worn out cot beds and an even worse off teenage girl. Another Aura female she vaguely recognized from a Resistance meeting awhile back.

Renata had only gotten a few words out before the Vampires came to drag her away. She'd been thrown in a shower and woken up here. Her skin still raw from the heat of the water, her hair still damp judging by the occasional trickles of water that dripped from her curls and tickled her neck and the bare skin of her shoulders.

Naked and tied up? Look where you landed yourself now, you big jerk.

Renata began to chastise herself. She jumped as hands gripped her shoulders from behind.

"Shh, I am just here to make sure you are okay," a soft female voice said.

Renata felt the woman's energy reach out to her. In a moment of relief, Renata let her own energy flow and mingle with the other woman's. At least, until she felt the same darkness that got her here in the first place. The woman was Aura but tainted.

How?

Renata wasn't sure she could trust anyone at this point, not even herself. She pulled her energy back. Afraid of what would happen next. The woman's hands left her shoulder.

"This one will do, the others are less knowledgeable," the woman said, and suddenly new hands were on Renata.

She struggled despite being bound, but it was no use. She was carried out of the room she was in, the ticking of the clock fading away like the false hope the other woman had given her just moments before.

"No! No! No," Renata cried through the gag.

"Don't fight it. It will be worse for you if you do," the woman said.

Another wave of calming energy settled over Renata. Enough to force her into a more docile state. Renata wanted to throttle whoever this Aura was but was unable to do anything more than comply with the woman's wishes. Renata's ankles were freed, and she was placed on the ground.

A soft rug beneath her feet, some kind of animal fur if her toes were correct. A rush of air hit her face, and she coughed as her nostrils were overwhelmed with cigar smoke. She was pushed forward roughly, and she carefully took one step then another. Her stomach twisted, and sweat dripped down her naked frame like the tickling of spider legs. She moved just a few steps at a time around in a circle.

"Ring around the rosie, trapped me like a poser, ashes, ashes, I'm so dead now."

Renata sang her morbid little tune the entire parade around the room. She heard vague hmms and awws as she passed what she assumed to be people. She didn't dare use her energy again at this point. She was pushed in a different direction and forced to stand still. Her ankles were rebound, and her blindfold removed. Not that it mattered. The room was dark, except for the spotlight trained on her naked body.

That's it. I'm dead. I'm going to die.

She stood there, bile rising in her throat, legs and arms cramping, jaw tight, choking back a scream. Tears streamed down her face. She noticed a sign above her head. Numbers flashed in rapid succession, going up and up. Renata felt faint but too afraid to actually pass out. She was being auctioned.

This isn't happening. This is all a really fucked up dream. Wake Up! Wake Up! Wake Up!

Frantically, Renata searched for a way out, some kind of weapon, a blunt object, anything to end this nightmare. She jerked forward only to find she was chained to the floor.

Fuck! Fuck! Fuck!

Glancing at the numbers again, her stomach flipped and knotted. She couldn't believe the numbers she saw. Millions were being spent on her for Horus only knew what.

Time

The bright sun filtered through partially opened blinds. Mack rolled over with a groan, letting the sun cast its rays on his back instead of directly across his eyes. He snuggled into the soft pillow before he registered Disrayan's scent heavy in the air. It took a moment for his exhaustion fogged brain to register that, one, he was not in his own bed, and two, while her soft floral scent and energy were everywhere, Disrayan herself was not. Mack sat up and blinked a few times.

The bedroom was exactly the same as he remembered. The light shade of purple Disrayan had painted the walls to remind them of the Ceresian sky, the soft taupe of the bedding to remind her of the basic tent she grew up in. An old alarm clock sat on her side of the bed, the soft ticking of its mechanism a reminder that he was on borrowed time. Instead of the framed photo from their Binding Announcement, his old nightstand was glaringly bare. A reminder that he was no longer a fixture in her life.

Mack leaned against the tufted headboard and sighed. For a moment, he let himself reminisce about the good days. When he'd have woken to Disrayan already up and dressed, complaining about him leaving his boxers on the bathroom floor as she completed her morning routine. He would lounge in bed a few minutes longer, enjoying the view of her long legs and heart-shaped ass as she reached for the mouthwash. He always put it on the top shelf above the sink just so he could see her suit skirt rise up the backs of her thighs, or if it was the week-end, one of his shirts.

It didn't matter how many times he'd seen her naked, it was the highlight of his day. That last little tease before she would chastise him for running behind schedule and head into the kitchen to make them coffee and toast with butter. Rye wasn't a bad cook; she just didn't see the point in making a fuss over daily meals. Especially if that meant carving extra time out of her busy schedule.

The buzzing of his phone took Mack from his memories. Disrayan had folded his clothes neatly and placed them on the black wood dresser. Of course, she had. Disrayan hated disorder. She organized and planned like nobody's business. She'd even planned every detail of their courtship.

Mack's life was anything but orderly. To be honest, the only constant in his life right now, other than his job at Club Obelisk, was the sharp ache where his heart should be. Left there by the regret he held that he couldn't be the man Disrayan wanted him to be. Couldn't offer her the stability and peace of mind she craved. At least, not right now.

He got out of bed, the soft pile of the carpet massaging his feet as he walked to the dresser. Not many people had his number, and of those few, only two would dare call him this early. Unfortunately, it wasn't Molly with a crisis at the nightclub. It was Commander Mars.

"Morning, Commander," Mack answered, trying his best to not sound as exhausted as he felt.

When the Commander of the Magelor Security Force first

approached him with the top-secret assignment, Mack nearly laughed in the man's face. Leave his family, leave Disrayan behind and go undercover monitoring Vampires? That was a suicide mission if Mack ever heard one, but then the Commander explained and showed him in the original texts the story of Maura and the havoc she created. The commander gave him the names and photos of her minions, as well as a list of their many crimes. The evidence of Maura's return and what that could mean for everyone, including the Aura, was what changed Mack's mind. Not even Ceres would be safe if she regained her power and completed what she began many years ago.

"Maclovis, I'm sure you are aware of the situation with the gate, but it will make communicating that much harder right now. What's the update?" Commander Mars said.

"Maura continues to gain strength and numbers, but remains untraceable. Still, no evidence that the targets are working with or for her. I think it's safe to say they may handle the Maura situation for us, if given a chance. They subdued her once before. Who's to say they won't do it again?" Mack replied.

"Who is to say they won't join ranks with her if she becomes powerful enough? We can't take any chances. I chose you because you wouldn't get caught up in the details. You are a big picture sort of man. I like that. Don't make me question your judgment now. Too much is at stake," the Commander said.

"No, sir. I will keep watch and report to you on schedule at the end of the week," Mack confirmed before he ended the call.

He took another look around the room and spotted the smudged purple paint just above the headboard. The paint hadn't fully dried when he'd pressed Disrayan's ass against the wall while sheathed fully inside her. He only managed to get her to keep the mark because it resembled a heart. A symbol of their love right above where they would lay together as husband and wife. Mack shook his head. Where they would have if he hadn't taken the mission to protect the world from the evils of Maura.

His gaze traveled back to the empty nightstand. His brain filling in the missing pieces. His leather valet, a glass of water, but most importantly, that framed photo of him and Disrayan. Both a few years younger, bright smiles on their faces. Mack's looked at least ten years younger with his red brown locks in a thick braid down his back, his golden skin alight with the joy of love as he looked into Disrayan's warm chocolate eyes. Her perfectly shaped bob framing her high cheekbones with full lips that begged to be kissed. Caught in the moment, Mack remembered how flawless and buttery soft her chestnut skin felt under his fingertips as he pulled her in to do just that. She'd felt the same last night in the throes of passion, but it was different now. In that moment, he'd been filled with so much joy, so much hope for their future together, but that was gone. Mack had even cut off his locks, not only to change his appearance for the job, but as penance for screwing up the best thing he had going in his life.

Mack got dressed and left Disrayan's apartment. She wouldn't want to see him there when she returned, even if he could have stayed. Last night had been amazing, but he wouldn't pretend that spending a night having angry sex resolved their issues. Not by a long shot. He hated that he couldn't come clean to her about why he left, but his job wasn't finished. He couldn't put her in danger, and last night couldn't happen again. Not until he finished his assignment, and by then, who knew. She may hate him even more.

...

Disrayan made her way through the familiar maze of stalls

and tents that ringed the Meeting House. The purple hue of the sky both familiar and troublesome. Ceres was falling, and not just because of the issues with the Barrier. For Disrayan, it had ceased to be a sanctuary a long time ago, but it would take time for the rest of the citizens to see that. Time they didn't have.

"Blessed be, Magistrate!" A burly man nodded at Disrayan from his squatted position.

He was in the midst of hammering in a stake for one of the refugee tents.

"Blessed be," Disrayan replied.

She didn't stop to chat. Her mind too busy processing the unfamiliar sights before her. The dense fog obscured the top level of the Meeting House from view. A scattering of men bustled about setting up tents in any available space to house the Aura who had lost their homes in the recent disaster. The Barrier shrunk so rapidly that people were forced to flee, leaving behind their belongings. Refugees in Ceres, the thought was still so foreign. Hushed whispers from inside a newly erected tent caught Disrayan's attention.

"To hell with this mess. We need to close the gate and reinforce the Barrier," a man said.

She slowed her pace to catch more snippets of the man's grumbling. The mob at the Meeting House expressed great displeasure with how the gate issue was being handled, but this was a chance to get details that could benefit her in her case. If there was any way to soften the feelings toward the Ruling Council, she would need to use that in her pursuit to clear Hendrex's name.

"What do you think will happen next?"

"Damned if I know. Nothing good for sure," another man said.

"The Ruling Council need to get their heads out of their asses and fix this mess."

Their pessimism didn't bode well. She could hardly blame them though, given the state of things.

"Not all the Ruling Council, Ruling Three is the only one I trust to settle this matter."

There were grunts of approval that made Disrayan's blood boil. Ruling Three was the last person to solve the issue with the Barrier. In fact, Disrayan wasn't entirely sure the man hadn't caused the issue himself. If there were more elders around, then it would be known that the Barrier shrinking wasn't new.

Ceres had once been a vast land, but the last few decades saw it shrinking away inch by inch. Those at the edge of the so-called paradise had seen their gardens slip away and were forced to move their tents at least once to be farther from the shrinking edges. It just so happened that this instance occurred in a matter of minutes, swallowing several yards into the void without warning.

"There has to be a way to fix this," Disrayan muttered to herself.

Her mind reeled with everything that had happened the last few days. Finding the missing Aura teen, uncovering an Aura trafficking operation run by Vampires, the gate to Ceres closing, the near death of Ceres itself, and the ensuing panic that prompted the political turmoil she now had to sort out. That, on top of reuniting with Maclovis. The thought of Mack lounging in her bed when she returned temporarily distracted her from the chaos around her.

Was she ready to forgive him completely? Maybe not, but the last few days were a start. Her body tingled with excitement at the thought of returning home to warm sheets and soft caresses. She bit her lip to keep her soft moan of need at bay. She shook her head and gazed directly ahead. Now was not the time to get caught up in personal matters.

A child's whimpering drew her attention to her left. A lump caught in her throat as she saw a mother doing her best to calm her young daughter. Soft light danced in her palm in the shape of a deer. The child's face lit up, and for a moment, she was distracted by the dire situation at hand. Disrayan wished someone would take the time to show her the light. Some beacon of hope, but Disrayan knew it was up to her to find that for herself. A lesson she'd learned when she was not much older than the young child in front of her.

The Barrier's weakness was not a passing issue. Something had to be done. They were lucky no lives were lost. That no one had been traveling through the gate at the moment of failure. That the alarm sounded almost immediately; another detail that was suspect. It had been a long time since Disrayan had been an investigator before she accepted the apprenticeship of the Magistrate. Even still, something about the incident didn't feel right.

Disrayan sighed. She didn't have time to follow up on any conspiracy theories her head chose to cook up in the moment. She needed to take a look at the historical record for any precedence for a case such as the one she'd stepped into. As far as she knew, it was unheard of for a member of the Ruling Council to publicly accuse another of a crime. How was she supposed to proceed without treading the dangerous lines of politics? As Magistrate, she was supposed to be impartial. She did technically work for the Ruling Council, but until now, their jurisdiction over her and how she proceeded hadn't been an issue. The Ruling Council had always presented a united front for the good of the people. Right now, they were showing to be anything but.

Disrayan circled back to the Meeting House. The Archives were in a smaller building attached to the Meeting House. Once inside she found the large tome that held the original contract between the founding families, as well as subsequent changes. She'd all but memorized the thing while in training, but it never hurt to give something a second pair of eyes. Maybe she could find a way to end this without further public spectacle.

The Aura deserved better than the disturbing show of mob justice she narrowly quelled. At least, she thought they did. The Aura of Ceres were so concerned with the injustice of the outside world. They had lived peacefully in fear of becoming the very thing that forced them into hiding. The lessons of the elders had worn thin, and Ruling Three was capitalizing on the mass hysteria the Barrier incident had caused. It was now up to Disrayan to remind everyone what Aura culture was truly about. To restore the sense of community and family she herself relied on during the trials of her life.

Disrayan manipulated the energy of the candle that sat on the table. Normally, it would be light enough in the tent to read, but the dense fog that hung over Magelor blocked the Barrier's light source. She watched the flame flicker to life, casting dancing shadows along the large oak table it sat upon. She fought the momentary panic that rose in her chest. Fire had taken her family away from her. She spent years learning to master its energy properties to ensure that she would never again be afraid. Maybe it was the atmosphere and the unsettling events of the last few nights that had her on edge. Either way, Disrayan needed to get her wits about her and quick. The future of Ceres and Aura culture were at stake. A daunting task, to say the least. One she was prepared to risk everything to accomplish.

Forbidden

Jaquis Andromeda took a look around before sneaking out the back door of Enora's condo. Even when she wasn't home to chastise him, he still didn't dare break her rules for their late-night encounters. It was bad enough he stuck around to the morning light. He slept like a baby on her super soft mattress with bright floral sheets. A stark contrast to the sterile decor of the rest of her home. A window into her more delicate side.

The coast was clear, no one would see him leaving her home. Not that anyone should care. They were both grown and consenting adults. Then again, she was a Security Force Officer, and he was arguably an enemy of Ceres as the leader of The Resistance. Once safely on the main streets and out of Enora's neighborhood, Jaq pulled out his phone.

He shot Enora a text saying he locked up her place and to hit him up later for a replay. He tried not to be offended when she didn't immediately answer. It wasn't like Enora was the only woman in his inbox, but she was the only one that mattered.

He was about to put his phone away when a new notification sprung up from his second in command, Jasmine.

"Gate has reopened. I set a meeting to discuss what happened and how we can use it to further our message."

Jaq smiled and shot a text back that he would meet her in ten at the usual place. The gate being closed for so long was a big deal. The Aura outside of Ceres felt even more abandoned by the Ruling Council than usual. It was prime time for recruitment, and yet he'd spent the last few days drowning himself in carnal pleasures with Enora. Thankfully, Jasmine and her partner Jasper were on top of things in his absence.

"About time you showed up," Jasper grumbled as Jaq joined them at the café where they occasionally held organization meetings.

Jasper had much more militant ideas about how The Resistance should handle business. Jaq wasn't really a fan of the guy, but he did have his uses. Particularly, his general lack of trust and paranoia. Both made him key in keeping their members safe during meetings. A new source of stress now that it was clear his group was targeted as a hunting ground for rogue Vampires and the blood slave racket. That shit had to stop immediately.

"Yeah, yeah. What did I miss?"

"The gate closure was a bigger issue than we thought. Apparently, the Barrier itself malfunctioned. Ceres has shrunk by at least twenty-five percent, displacing more of the Aura population. The gate is reopened but only for official travel. People are losing it, both in and out of the Sanctuary. We've seen a major influx of interest in joining our cause and taking on the Ruling Council. To be proactive about a permanent solution to the stability of Ceres," Jasmine said.

"So, the rumors of routine maintenance are officially debunked?"

"I mean, that's the statement that was given initially by the Ruling Council until Ruling Three released his own statement. He claims the constant traveling between worlds is weakening the Barrier."

Jaq nodded his head. He didn't like what he was hearing. Ruling Three had always been a shifty bastard. Jaq held no love for the Ruling Council, but Ruling Three had a particular ick factor about him that very few others seemed to acknowledge. Nothing good could come from that man, even if it meant The Resistance would now have more manpower in the fight against the establishment.

"My sources say the Barrier failing wasn't an accident. We aren't the only ones who aren't satisfied with the status quo. This was an inside job," Jasper said.

Jaq rolled his eyes, but Jasper's explanation sounded more plausible than the official statement of routine maintenance gone wrong.

"What source would that be, the Aura underground?"

"No, the Aura on duty the night of the incident just happened to be my cousin," Jasper snapped.

Jaq leaned forward, intrigued by this new information.

"Alright, tell me what you know."

...

Disrayan closed the massive leather-bound tome she'd been reading and rubbed her eyes. Between the dim light of the candle and the intricately scrawled handwriting, her vision had started to blur and a dull ache formed between her eyes. It was time to call it quits. Light was fading with the coming night, and the new gate curfew meant she needed to leave now or risk crashing her best friend's courtship to get a quiet place to sleep.

Disrayan shook her head. She'd maintained her grandparents' tent after their passing specifically for nights like this. When work required late hours of studying. It had been her home after her parents and siblings passed away. The only place left in this world with mostly happy memories for her, and now it was gone. The small tent had been her little getaway on the far edges of Ceres. Farther than most dared to wander, most wanting to be as close to Magelor as possible. Her family home was now lost to the void. Along with all of her grandmother's woven blankets and her grandfather's hand-carved furniture.

A lone tear fell from Disrayan's face. Even when her Grandmother had passed, her last living relative, Disrayan hadn't felt this alone. Shaking the painful thought away, she wiped the tear from her face. This was not the time or the place to be emotional. Ceres might be paradise to some, but it was hell for someone like Disrayan who prioritized her right to privacy. It was the main reason she moved from Ceres. That, and to be closer to Maclovis.

Disrayan wondered if he was still at her place. If he'd stayed in bed all day, or if he'd moved to the couch to binge watch human TV before work like when he had lived there with her. Then again, that was when he actually cared about something other than himself. He obviously hadn't cared much about her, but that was the least of her problems with him. She recognized the drastic shift in her thinking from earlier. Now that her emotions had settled, and she had time to really think. Disrayan honestly didn't want him to be there when she got home.

The previous nights were a calamity of mixed emotions. They meant nothing when it came to rekindling some sort of relationship with him, despite the fact it was the third night she found herself calling him to her bed. The first night happened right after they dropped off the missing girls. Emotions were high then, so she gave herself a pass for that. The second night was right after the first, before they knew the gate situation. It had been easy to dismiss him after that.

As Magistrate, it was imperative she remained in contact with Ceres to ensure those outside of Ceres things were under control. Even though they weren't. Yet, last night, after an exhausting day of fielding questions from the masses, she found herself dialing the number he'd left on the side of the bed. Mack arrived within minutes of her call. And once he came, well, it wasn't long before she had many, many arrivals of her own.

Disrayan did her best to focus on the task at hand. She didn't need this kind of confusion. Especially not now. It was best if he wasn't waiting when she returned home. Disrayan wasn't sure she could continue to keep her old emotions at bay. Although, if he was there it would make things easier when it came to delivering the summons from the Ruling Council. Disrayan got up from the wooden bench and stretched her arms wide, bending side to side to relieve some of the tension in her lower back.

Ceres, for all the advancements they had made over the years, was in dire need of an upgrade. There were so many great things about the human world that they purposefully refused to integrate under the guise of "retaining Aura culture." It was a load of garbage as far as Disrayan was concerned. It wasn't that she didn't see a reason to be concerned with the loss of Aura culture. As more families left the safety of Ceres, the youth were more likely to adopt human culture as their own. It wouldn't hurt to build more permanent dwellings than tents if it was still safe to stay in Ceres. Certain concessions needed to be made either way. There were still plenty of Aura who had never stepped outside the Barrier. Had never seen a real brick building, or one more than three stories high. It was one thing to preserve one's culture, but quite another to actively censure another to do so.

So many would be completely out of depth in the human

world if they needed to evacuate Ceres for good. Keeping their culture would be the least of their problems at that point. Disrayan stepped out of the Archives building and into the market encircling the Meeting House.

The streets were just as deserted as earlier. Most having gone home to their sleeping tents. It was already dark, and not just because of the time but also the low hanging fog caused by the Barrier's malfunction. Disrayan could see the soft glow of cooking hearths in the distance, and she headed toward them. Not because she wished to join any of the community for a meal, but because it was on the way to the Garden Gate path. The path once open to all was now lined with Security Force Officers. Each pair about ten feet from each other.

Disrayan nodded at them as she walked by until she reached the final pair at the end of the path.

"State your reasons for leaving," one of the guards barked.

Disrayan fought the urge to roll her eyes. It had been Ruling One's decision to restrict use of the Garden Gate, of course only from inside the Sanctuary.

"I wish to return to my home," Disrayan said.

The guard frowned before looking at the other questioningly.

"She's the Magistrate," the other muttered before quickly drawing the Runes to open the gate and allow her through.

"Thank you," she said and nodded at the reasonable officer before stepping through.

The trip lasted several seconds. Disrayan took a moment for her head to stop spinning before she could hazard another step. It hadn't been that hard of a trip earlier in the day when the gate first opened. Maybe the Ruling Council was right to restrict travel through the gate. If she could help it, Disrayan would avoid traveling through as much as possible.

Her body couldn't handle that much turmoil every day. She made note to have a light breakfast in the morning, so as not to embarrass herself after the trip back. She knew she would have to return tomorrow to finish her search, which was bad enough. Disrayan wasn't exactly sure what she was looking for, but she knew the massive histories held the key to whatever the hell was going on with the Ruling Council and the Barrier.

Tested

Hendrex retreated back to his office and away from madness in the Meeting Hall. He'd done his best to assure the people that homes would be provided to them and a solution would be had before the week's end. The latter was a long shot as the Ruling Council couldn't come to agreement about the best course of action. He left frustrated that once again the other Ruling Council members were proving to be more about personal politics than achieving a consensus for the greater good. Openly bickering in front of the people wasn't something Hendrex would do. Whatever Ruling Three planned, the man had surely succeeded in dividing the council.

Standing in front of his baseball memorabilia, Hendrex shook his head. At one point, he'd dreamed of being on a professional team. No one but Zarovia knew he used to sneak out of lessons to go to a local youth league practice. He'd been good enough to catch a few coaches' eyes, but he never got the chance to see just how far he could go. As he'd gotten older and questions about his schooling came up, he said he was homeschooled, which wasn't a lie. He did attend school at home in Ceres, but they couldn't know that. They had wanted him to attend their human schools and play on the school team.

When he'd brought the idea to his father, Hendrex thought the old man was going to have a heart attack. He went on and on about how cursed he was to have a son so void of energy, and another intent on putting himself in danger in the human world. Hendrex gave up on his dream that day. Hendrex had given up a lot to please his father. To prove he wasn't a disappointment, and for what? To be publicly ridiculed and charged with a most heinous crime? Not for the first time Hendrex envied his twin Maclovis for the freedom he demanded. Envied Mack's ability to walk away from it all—the expectation, the responsibility, the literal weight of the world.

Their father was no longer in this life to see what a disgrace Hendrex was becoming to the Andromeda name. Not that it held much clout with the antics of his brother and cousins. He was the only one concerned with the great ruling tradition. A flare came from behind the closed door of his office. He recognized Donovan's strong energy and flared his own in response.

The door opened carefully, and Donovan came in alone. A feat in itself considering Donovan had recently coerced Farrah into a Binding Ceremony. He should have been off enjoying the celebration of their impending union. Then again, Donovan was a man of duty. Like Hendrex, he too carried the weight of his family's name and status. Business always came before personal pursuits for men like them.

"I hope Farrah is aware of this visit, otherwise, I wish you luck upon your return to her side," Hendrex said.

Donovan smiled.

"She's too busy arguing with her mother about the celebration details to notice I've slipped away. I just wanted to give you a full report on the information we gathered during our mission the other night," Donovan said.

"Right, I am glad you kept the news light during the proceedings, but I think this should be shared with all the Ruling Council," Hendrex said.

"I must respectfully disagree, Ruling Four. Given the information I have, I wouldn't want the others to rush to drastic decisions that would add to the current state of distrust and chaos," Donovan said.

Hendrex turned to face the man and nodded.

"Alright then, what have you learned?" Hendrex asked.

"I cannot confirm that the Secret of Ceres itself is safe, but I can say that there is an element amongst Vampires that are aware that we, the Aura, do still exist in the world. They are targeting our young women and selling them to the highest bidder. The purpose of this is unknown, but I wish to continue my investigation and find out," Donovan said.

"That I must agree with. We need to be sure of the precise dangers we face. I cannot say that I am entirely surprised by the scare we received with the great Barrier. It is just a symptom of the larger issue. I had hoped we had more time, but I need as much information as soon as possible," Hendrex said.

"There is another matter, Ruling Four. One of a more personal matter," Donovan said.

Hendrex had never seen the man hesitant about anything, other than working with Farrah. It didn't help ease Hendrex's nerves not one bit.

"Yes," he prompted.

"Maclovis Andromeda aided us in the raid, and he enlisted the help of Vampires. They knew what we were and had no problem working with us against their own kind. I'm not sure if they were hired help, but that is something to be of concern. I know he is your brother, but I can't entirely say I trust his testimony to help in your situation," Donovan said.

Hendrex was touched that the man even cared. Then again, they would be family soon.

"Thank you, but Maclovis and I have cut ties long ago. If he even shows up to give testimony, I assure you it won't carry much weight," Hendrex said, and turned back to admiring his collection.

Hendrex saw Donovan bow from the corner of his eye, leaving Hendrex to his sulking. This whole situation was a mess, and for once in his life, Hendrex wasn't seeing a satisfactory outcome in his future.

...

A knot formed in Donovan's gut as he left Ruling Four in his office. Even the joy of Binding with Farrah couldn't shake the unease growing there. Ruling Three was definitely up to something, but Donovan couldn't focus on that right now. He made his report to Ruling Four about the underground auctions of helpless Aura. Now he needed to plan how to deal with the issue. Aura needed to maintain a presence in the human world. The issue was if they were truly safe to be there.

The Magelor Security Force needed a major change in policy to reflect the changes of the human world. The evolution of the very real threat of Vampires. Donovan needed help in shoring up alliances with the other supernatural in the area to help keep the Aura safe. As much as he hated to admit it, he needed Jaquis' help. Being the leader of The Resistance, Jaq undoubtedly had allies and knowledge that would be indispensable in the task of ensuring the safety of the Aura moving forward.

Donovan made his way back to the Meeting Room. Farrah was no longer there. She'd been cornered by his mother and hers as soon as word got out about her agreement to Bind with him. He smiled thinking of the angry glare she shot his way when he slipped out of the room. Farrah would surely make him pay for leaving her alone with the two gushing women. He only hoped it would be in the bedroom and not on the sparring mat. During the few days they spent alone, Donovan learned that Farrah was quite adept at wrestling, as well as kick boxing.

Just the thought of those long legs of hers swinging up, stopping just before her dainty red painted toes collided with his jaw. He bit his lip remembering how he grabbed her ankle and pulled her closer. Hooking her leg around his neck before lifting her from the ground and burying his face between her legs. His manhood pressed against the inseam of his slacks, making him both curse and rejoice that he wore the denim pants that humans referred to as jeans, his Security Officer Uniform would have shown just how much he missed his partner in that moment.

"Donovan." He turned to see his father standing on the other side of the room.

He hoped the stern look on his father's face was an indication of a man to man talk about the commitment a Binding, but Donovan knew better. This was about the family business of ensuring the safety of Ceres. He straightened and forced the thought of Farrah from his brain. He didn't want to add a lecture on distractions to the list of talks his father was sure to give him.

"Yes, sir."

His father glanced around the room before Donovan felt his energy wrap around them. He recognized it as a sound dampening sphere. It was a technique his father used when speaking to his mother about things he hadn't wanted Donovan or his brother to hear growing up.

"I want you to continue working on this trafficking case. This mess with the Ruling Council is a distraction to the real issue at hand, and I need proof the human world is a viable option for our people if things get as bad as it looks to get."

Donovan frowned at his father. There was real fear beneath his words. It shook Donovan to the core.

"I already planned to do so. Is there something more I should know?"

The commander looked like he wanted to say more but instead shook his head.

"Just take care around the Vampires, son. Not all of them will be so easily handled."

With that the commander walked away, his energy receding in his wake. Feeling completely unbalanced, Donovan reached out for Farrah. He needed her now more than ever. She wouldn't have left Ceres without letting him know and couldn't have gotten far. He followed her pull until he found her in the Archives with Disrayan. Donovan should never have underestimated the power of Farrah's best friend. Disrayan had more than proved herself, not just in the Meeting Room, but that horrific night at the monster house. He was glad Farrah had such good friends to back her up when the time called for it. They would need that in the dark times ahead.

...

Disrayan set her phone aside for the third time with an audible sigh.

Don't do it, Rye, he isn't worth it.

She sank further into the tub, pink frothy bubbles sliding up to just above her chin; she stopped before the nape of her neck touched the water. She wanted to relax, not add more work to her already hectic routine by wetting her hair.

She closed her eyes and took a deep breath. The rose scented suds were usually all she needed to relax after a rough day, but now her body craved something else. She slid her hand between her thighs, parting the lips at her core as she touched herself.

Don't think of Mack, don't think of Mack.

Disrayan tried to focus on the image of a shirtless action star, but the deep umber of her actor of choice faded to an all too familiar caramel hue. Slowly sliding her fingers along her clit, the sensitive nub sprang to life. Swelling and tingling more with each stroke until she reached her peak. Yet, as her orgasm crested, it faltered spectacularly, leaving her both breathless and even more frustrated.

With a groan, she snatched her hand away from herself and sat up in the water. It was no use. Her body wanted what her heart knew better than to crave. She grabbed her phone and dialed Mack's cell. It rang once, twice, and then she hung up. Tossing her phone onto a nearby towel, she pulled herself from the water.

Idiot! What are you going to do when he calls back? If he calls back?

She quickly rinsed off under the cool spray of her shower; she could have waited until the water warmed up, but in a way, it was her punishment for not being able to just forget about Mack. He had managed to weasel his way back in after all this time. Disrayan was just stepping out of the shower when there was a knock at the front door. She quickly grabbed her robe and tossed it on before heading to the door. She wasn't expecting a package or anything, so maybe it was one of the girls coming to hang out and decompress from all the drama as of late.

What Disrayan didn't expect was for Mack to be standing on her front porch. He took one look at her still dripping wet in her robe and wasted no time pushing himself inside. Slamming the door behind him, Mack swept Disrayan into his arms, kissing away whatever protest she could have uttered at his not so unwelcome intrusion.

"I was hoping you'd call," Mack muttered between kisses.

"It was an accident. I meant to call Farrah," Disrayan lied.

Letting her robe fall open, Disrayan sank to the couch. Mack followed, unbuckling his pants along the way.

He smirked before capturing her taut nipple in his mouth. She moaned and arched her back.

"Liar, liar," he hissed.

Her breath caught at the warmth dancing over her now wet and sensitive flesh. Disrayan reached into his boxers and freed him from his confines. Hot and heavy in her grasp, she began to stroke him.

"Let's not make this into more than it has to be," she said before guiding him straight to her core.

Mack pressed into her until his hips were firmly pressed against hers. She tried to move her hips, desperate for the hot friction against her clit, but Mack held her firm, teasing her with little licks and nips across her chest.

"On the contrary, Rye. I plan to make this everything it could be."

She felt his energy reaching out to hers, beckoning her to meld her energy with his. Instead of allowing for the connection that would undoubtedly heighten the sexual experience between them, Rye used her energy to force him into a roll, placing herself on top as she took control of the situation.

"Rye, please."

She refused to look him in the eye, choosing only to focus on the building pleasure inside her as she rode him to release. His hand gripped her hips, guiding her into a slow grinding motion.

"Yes," she cried as her orgasm ripped through her.

She rode out the waves before collapsing onto Mack's chest. Her heavy breathing and the thumping of their heartbeats the only sound in the room for several minutes. Mack rubbed her back and pressed a kiss to her forehead.

"I don't mind being a booty call for now, Rye, but eventually we will have to talk about what this means."

Disrayan sat up and looked at him. The warmth is his eyes told her that he meant it, but Disrayan wasn't ready to go all in on whatever was happening with them right now. She bent over and kissed his lips gently before getting up and heading for the bedroom. She turned around when she realized he wasn't following her.

"Are you not coming?"

Mack sighed and pulled himself off the floor. For a moment, it looked like he was going to bail on her, but then a slow smile crept onto his face before he lunged for her. With a yelp, Disrayan ran with Mack dogging her heels. He caught up to her easily, sweeping her into his arms before tossing her onto the bed.

"Oh, I definitely plan to come," he growled before settling over her body once more.

...

"I can't believe you are back in here! Did you even sleep last night?

Disrayan looked up from the book she was reading to glare at Farrah.

"I'm trying to do my job and keep your cousin from being

stripped of his title and banished," Disrayan snapped.

"Touchy, I guess Mack didn't work all the kinks out last night, huh?"

Disrayan chose to glare at the book of laws instead of giving Farrah the satisfaction of seeing her embarrassment.

"I have no idea what you are talking about," she muttered.

"Oh, Come on, Rye. I'm really good at reading people, and the last time your energy was this balanced, you and Mack were attached at the hip. Although, judging by the hostile energy, maybe not totally back together," Farrah said.

"How many times have I told you not to read people without asking?" Disrayan snapped.

"I'm a private investigator. It's within my rights to snoop. Especially, when it's key to an active case," Farrah said.

Disrayan looked at Farrah curiously.

"How am I part of your active case?"

"You helped rescue those women, and you rode with them to the hospital. Tell me. Did they talk to you about what happened to them? Give you any clues about what happened to the other girls? Or were you too busy balancing your energy with Mack to get anything useful?" Farrah said sitting on the edge of the table in front of Disrayan.

Farrah leaned in until Disrayan became uncomfortable with the breach of her private space. Farrah was lucky she was one of Disrayan's best friends, otherwise, she wouldn't have tolerated the breach.

"The women were traumatized and understandably silent in the midst of two giant Vampires. Most of them spent their time crying and didn't linger for pleasantries when we dropped them at the hospital," Disrayan said.

"Damn, I hoped you had something good. I mean, I get that they went through something horrible, but Donovan is already shutting me out of the investigation. I was hoping you would have a lead for me to go on," she said.

"Your future husband has a right to protect you and keep you out of trouble. I'm sure if your help is needed, he will reach out. In the meantime, can I get back to the important matter of saving the dignity and efficacy of the Ruling Council?"

Farrah scowled at Disrayan before standing with a sigh.

"Fine, but just know I'm totally cool with you forgiving Mack, you know, if that's a thing again," she said before sashaying dramatically out of the tent.

Disrayan knew it wasn't for her benefit. She turned to see Donovan leaning against the doorway to the Meeting House.

"I was just coming to ask about the women we saved, but Farrah has obviously saved me the trouble," he grumbled.

Disrayan smiled at her friend's fiancé and waved him over to where she sat.

"She's persistent. You'll either admire it or cope with it."

"Which one do you do?"

"Cope, obviously. Farrah is an amazing woman, and I am grateful to call her my friend, even when she's nosey," Disrayan said.

Donovan laughed, and for the first time, Disrayan got a glimpse of what Farrah must see in him. Not that he wasn't good looking, but in previous encounters with him, Donovan had seemed so uptight. Too unyielding to put up with Farrah's wild style of living. Even yesterday, he'd swooped in and left with Farrah without so much as a "hey, how are you." Then again, he was probably trying to get Farrah alone to celebrate their impending Binding and blow off some steam. Yesterday had been a rough day for everyone, which had led to her poor decision to call Mack. Donovan stopped laughing and pegged Disrayan with a serious look. The abrupt switch in tone brought Disrayan back to the present situation and not her weakness for another Andromeda.

"On a more serious note, thank you for stepping in back there. I have no idea what's going on with the Ruling Council, but I'm glad you were there before it became even more of a shit show," Donovan said.

"Shit show? Wow, Farrah really has made an impression on you," Disrayan said with a laugh.

Donovan's intense gaze didn't falter, nor did any humor light his features like before. Disrayan cleared her throat and shuffled around the books in front of her.

"It's no problem at all. I was just doing my job. There are rules in place for this very reason. Law and order will be maintained as long as I am within means and power to uphold it,'" she said,

Donovan nodded.

"Anyway, if you remember anything that may be of use, please feel free to contact me."

"Will do."

"Good to hear," Donovan stood to leave, "I will keep you informed of anything pertinent to the trafficking case. Blessed be and merry met, Disrayan."

She watched as Donovan walked out of the Archives and shook her head. Farrah was one lucky girl.

Mack opened the door to his small apartment a few blocks away from his job at Club Obelisk. The sun was about to rise, and he felt exhausted. Working at the club to keep an eye on Molly and the rest of Maura's progeny took up the majority of his waking hours. The rest, he spent in a lonely haze of memories and what ifs. Nights with Rye also took up a considerable amount of his mental capacity recently. As much as he would love to rekindle things with her, he hadn't finished his job yet. His job was important. Not just to him, but for the safety of his people. Maura was not just a fairy tale like his people thought. She was real, all too real, and more of a threat than even Commander Mars knew.

She was a bigger threat than even the Vampire Council. Although Mack wouldn't want to cross paths with them, either. He'd heard rumors of Magic Wielders being coveted by Vampires because they thought their blood would make them more powerful. Coveted, but never actually captured. Now after helping Donovan and Farrah save that Aura girl. He wasn't so sure the Vampire Council was so easily written off either.

Mack was treading in some very dangerous waters. The only benefit being his rare dark energy. It protected him from being read as anything more than human, unless the person reading him knew what they were doing or happened to be a shifter. Mack shivered thinking of his first encounter with one of those. Yet another so called myth of his people. One would think all of these things would make Maclovis pray for the day he could return to the safety of Ceres. Only Ceres wasn't the safe haven it was meant to be. Not just with the issues with the Barrier, but whispers of the civil unrest had already traveled the Aura gossip circuit.

No doubt propagated by The Resistance. A group of young kids and outcast adults who railed against the system, just to get a rise from their parents, or to justify their lack of self-esteem. Speaking of, Mack kicked the lump of blankets in the middle of his living room floor. It groaned before shifting and Mack's cousin Jaq peered out from the mass.

"What the hell is your problem?"

Mack shook his head.

"You get kicked out of your place again?" Mack asked.

Jaq sighed and sat up.

"Nah, just laying low until this kidnapping stuff blows over," Jaq said.

"Explains why you're on my floor and not at your sister's."

"Farrah's always got my back, it's Mars I'm avoiding. You think she's really going to let him court her?" Jaq said.

Mack ran a hand down his face. He was tired and didn't have the time or patience for his cousin's drama.

"Beats me, you see how I'm living," Mack said, hoping the self-deprecating statement would get him off the hook.

"Yeah, you really fucked up with Rye. Anyway, you hear about the Gate being closed?"

Jaq apparently wasn't going to take a hint, but the Security Officer in Mack couldn't resist getting details about what exactly the leader of The Resistance knew about the crisis and what his plans were. Mack would never investigate his own cousin. Jaq, although misguided, was genuine in his concern for Aura welfare. It was his so-called allies that didn't sit right with Mack.

"Yeah, but you know I don't get much detail about anything Aura related," Mack phished.

"Rumor has it that the Gate shutdown was done on purpose. That someone on the inside wanted to seal the Gate and go into seclusion without notifying anyone on the outside. Problem was they messed up the procedure and almost shut down the Barrier completely," Jaq said.

"That's crazy, I think your sources got like fifth hand news, man," Mack said.

"Nah, my boy is related to the guy who was on duty to regulate the energy flow. Says he was paid to swap shifts with someone. Deal was for him to step out five minutes before the swap, but when he got to the door, he forgot his book or something and went back," Jaq said.

"So, he just up and left his post without direct relief?"

"Dude was already pulling double shifts because they are short staffed. He figured five minutes couldn't do any harm."

"Who was supposed to relieve him? Do you know?"

"Nope, he claims no one was there when he went back up, but that the balancing crystals were off."

"I'm sure the Ruling Council will investigate," Mack said.

He didn't know that they would for sure, but at least they would look into who the guard's replacement could have been.

"More like not. They are too busy fighting each other to do anything. Another reason Ceres is doomed, and our people need to wake the fuck up and join the 21st century," Jaq muttered before laying back down.

"Well, I'm going to bed. You can have the couch for two more nights, but after that, you find another couch somewhere else," Mack said and went to his room.

He had a ton of sleep to catch up on considering he'd been

up most of the previous night with Rye. Mack adjusted himself as his body reacted to the thought of her. This is what Mack hoped to avoid. He didn't need her distracting him from his mission. He should never have gone to her last night, but he'd needed the release as much as Disrayan had. Two years without her, without sex, had really sucked. At least, it seemed that things with Maura were coming to a head. He just hoped it happened sooner rather than later. Now that he had another taste of Rye, he wasn't sure he could go too much longer without her.

Storyteller

"Don't give her too much! He will want to sample her immediately upon arrival," a female voice broke through the fog of Renata's barely conscious brain.

Her head tilted back, and her lips parted on their own. She knew she was already drugged. Her body felt limp and heavy, suspended in a half-woken state. Renata could hear and feel everything, but could do nothing to stop what was happening to her. A cool sweet liquid passed her lips. Gentle fingers rubbed her throat to ensure she swallowed.

The elixir warmed her throat the same as whatever drug had been slipped in her drink at Club Obelisk. Like a warm, fuzzy blanket, it settled through her body, blotting out her ability to call on the energy around her. She could still detect that it was there, but she couldn't reach it. Renata couldn't rely on the energies to help her in this situation.

Her head was released and fell against a soft pillow. Renata was no longer bound. Her arms were tucked neatly against her sides. A light blanket draped over her body. Refusing to open her eyes, Renata could only guess that she was in a bedroom. The energy she could detect was old and cared for. The same feeling she got from browsing antique stores on Sunday afternoons.

She felt the sheets being removed from her body. Gentle hands ran a warm wet cloth over her bare skin. She didn't fight it. She was too comfortable, at ease despite her unknown fate. It was a false feeling, but it was better than the panic and fear that shrank her to a quivering useless mess.

"That's it, relax. You will need your strength when meeting the master," the female voice whispered to her.

Renata had no idea who this woman was, but already she hated her. How could any woman willingly subject another to such inhumane treatment?

"My sister, if I could save you from this fate, I would, but I am tired and weak. I need your help to satisfy the master's appetite for Aura blood."

The words weren't spoken but played in her head.

"Save your shit excuses," Renata replied.

The woman had strong mind energy abilities, even drugged it wasn't an easy task to speak directly in someone else's head.

"Be grateful the master chose you. Sharing your blood is an intimate act, but the other buyers would have used you for your body as well."

"Just let me go. Say the elixir didn't work and I overpowered you."

The woman laughed, her voice like tinkling bells was piercing needles to Renata's sluggish brain.

"Why is she wincing? Don't try any stupid tricks," a brusque male voice said.

"Calm down, Brody. Your presence is probably alarming for her. She may be drugged, but she is powerful enough to still detect your devious energy," the woman answered aloud.

It made sense now why she spoke to Renata through her mental energy. They weren't alone in the room. Renata felt the woman push more calming energy her way. It settled her and cleared some of the drug induced fog.

"Watch your tongue, slave! Maximus may not care to touch you, but you know that doesn't mean you are entirely safe from bodily harm," the man snarled.

"Your threat may have worked a year ago, but now, I know better. The master prefers blood untainted by pain."

Renata wasn't sure she could trust this woman, but was slightly reassured that other than providing some undetermined amount of blood to her new owner, she would otherwise be safe. Well, as safe as any blood slave could be.

"Yes, but the master now has two of you. If she is as powerful as you say, he may no longer covet you as his favorite."

The woman didn't reply, but Renata felt a shift in the energy of the room. The woman was no longer so sure of herself. That didn't bode well for their budding connection. Renata would not be making friends with this woman. They were in this predicament together, but the Brody character had just thrown the gauntlet. Her only hope for an ally would now be her competition.

...

Mack sat in his car, tapping his thumbs on the steering wheel. An annoying nervous habit, but he couldn't stop himself. The thumping of flesh upon leather was soothing, like a heartbeat. Steady and rhythmic, unlike the beating of his own heart, which raced wildly to a cadence unknown to human kind.

Mack checked the digital display again. He had less than an hour drive to calm his frantic nerves.

Like tiny needle pricks just under the skin, the electric tension crept down his arms. The dusting of hair standing on end, his palms moist with perspiration, almost too slick to maintain control of the wheel. Mack needed to get a grip, but he couldn't shake the knowing. The 'knowing,' as he called it, was more a feeling. A deep sinking in his gut whenever something bad was about to happen. He had it the night Daphne disappeared and prior to learning that the Vampire Council would be paying Molly a visit.

He felt it again the night before the Gate to Ceres had sealed itself shut, and here it was again as he drove to the pristine coastal rehabilitation center to pick up Shane. He prayed it wasn't a warning about Shane, or worse, about Disrayan. All the crazy rumors going around the Aura community about the Gate and the Ruling Council had him on edge.

Mack shouldn't have torn up the summons. He should have gone and testified for his brother. Despite their differences, Mack held no ill will toward him. How could he when it was Hendrex who'd always shouldered the burden of Mack's otherness. It was Hendrex who took on the family burden when Mack chose to follow his calling. It was Hendrex who upheld the prestige of the Andromeda name while Mack and their cousins flitted about as they pleased.

Well, Mack hadn't flitted, but that didn't mean he hadn't off-loaded the most responsibility onto Hendrex. It had been Mack who ran from the nomination to Ruling Four, leaving Hendrex to take the mantel and continue the line of rule for the Andromeda family. Mack pressed the knob on the radio to turn it on. He usually drove in silence and enjoyed having nothing more than his own thoughts as company, but not today. He was too on edge. Something big was on the horizon. Something with the potential to change everything Mack had come to know.

He knew this as surely as he felt the twisting of his insides. Mack swerved and pulled the car to a stop. He yanked away his seatbelt and managed to open the car door in time to heave his lunch onto the pavement instead of his own lap. He was barely able to catch his breath. His eyes bulged with each heaving of his stomach; his vision began to blur as his brain was starved of much needed oxygen.

The darkness closed in fast, and with the last of his strength, Mack pushed back away from the door, closing it in time for the cool metal to catch his limp body. Mack forced shallow breaths into his lungs as the images came. A deep crimson hue tinged everything as if it had been steeped in blood. Energy crackled and sparked, hitting the ground, narrowly missing the crowds of people screaming in terror, clutching their loved ones. Pushing with all their might to break free from some invisible force that slowed their motion. The darkness, a deep black void, loomed in the distance. The landscape distorted by its overwhelming magnetism. The woman closest to him reached out her hand, and Mack reached for her. He wanted to help, needed to help, but the pull was too strong. The darkness enveloped them all.

Mack's eyes flew open immediately, and he gulped in the stale air of his stagnant vehicle. The taste of bile still on his tongue, it took a moment to get his bearings. He was safe in his car. The bright afternoon sun was beginning to set low on the horizon, casting a hazy glow to the trees and pavement in front of him. The engine of the car was still running, and where he once had almost a full tank, the needle now sat at the halfway mark.

Mack pulled his seatbelt on and hit the road. He didn't know how long he had been out, but he was definitely behind schedule. Mack checked the clock on the dash. Over an hour had passed. Mack had only had a vision like that once before, and it had been a much more pleasant. He'd had a vision of Disrayan smiling at him, a tiny bundle wrapped ever so carefully in her arms. He'd peered into the bundle to find bright eyes and tiny features that mimicked both his and Disrayan. The next day, he'd started the official Courtship with her.

If only he'd known then how things would be now. If he weren't already chilled to the bone, he would have been just thinking of the poor state of their relationship. That vision had yet to come true for them, and if this one was the same, maybe it would be merely a possible outcome of events. Either way, once Mack finished this errand for his Vampire friends, he would be taking on a different case. Maura could wait, especially if the fate of Ceres was at stake.

He pulled out his phone and dialed Jaq's number. When it rang three times, Mack cursed and almost hung up. It wouldn't be outside of Jaq's nature to have changed his phone number with everything that was going on. The man was notoriously hard to pin down. It was his personality that Mack had adopted in his undercover work. Mack was just about to hang up when Jaq answered.

"Hey man, what's up?" he huffed, his breath heavy like he'd just gone for a run, but the soft moan in the background told Mack otherwise.

"I need a favor."

"What kind of favor?"

"How good are your shifter contacts?"

...

The Meeting Room had finally emptied out, having acted as temporary shelter until all of the refugee tents had been prepared. The people of Ceres returned to their daily routine, more out of habit and a need for normalcy than a general ease with the Gate situation. Ruling One, Two, and Three were already waiting with stern looks on their faces as they stared each other down. Commander Mars stood guarding the main entry. This would be a private meeting, no angry mobs, no reason to hide one's true feelings on the matter. More time had passed for tempers to calm and rational thinking to actually occur. Hendrex hoped. This was how the situation with the Gate should have been handled in the first place. Not that dreadful display that did nothing but bolster the insecurities of the people.

"Well, look who finally decided to show up?" Ruling Three snarled.

Hendrex fought the urge to roll his eyes at the older man.

"I was receiving an update about the investigation you so imprudently outed," he replied instead.

"An investigation we all should have been aware of," Ruling One snapped.

"You would have been made aware if Ruling Three hadn't felt the need to undermine all of our authority with the people. It was merely an exploratory investigation as to the safety of the human realm. No matter what we decide for the people of Ceres, it was vital information to have," Hendrex said.

"Yes, necessary information that should have been shared prior to the investigation beginning. Instead, you chose to leave the Council out of it. I can only guess why? Maybe so you could skew the findings in your favor? For your own personal gain?"

Ruling Three stood directly in front of Hendrex, so close he could feel Ruling Three's breath on his face. Shrewd eyes stared into his own. There was no doubting the challenge there, the glint of excitement this drama brought Ruling Three.

"The only one with an obvious motive of self-gain is you, Ruling Three. Care to explain how you were so quick to sound the alarm about the Barrier, but so woefully late in meeting to discuss what that would mean for the Aura?"

The glint of excitement flickered with a devious flame.

"Don't try to distract from your own ill intent. You want to endanger our people by leaving the Sanctuary our ancestors provided. You live closest to the Meeting House, why wasn't it you who sounded the alarm? Perhaps, you wanted the people to suffer, for the Barrier to fall so you could force our people to the outside. To the whim of the humans and Vampires that you and your accomplices have befriended." Ruling Three was on a roll.

Hendrex clenched his fists at his sides.

"Save your baseless allegations for the trial," he ground out.

"Oh, I will." Ruling Three leaned closer and lowered his voice, "And once I'm done with you, I'll take care of that sweet Zarovia Monoceros in ways you have only dreamed."

Hendrex didn't notice he'd swung on the man until he was being pulled back by Commander Mars. Even with the massive age difference, the Commander was too strong for Hendrex to fight. Ruling Three smirked as Hendrex was dragged out of the Meeting Room seething. So much for his legendary control. Then again, no one had ever brought Zarovia up in that way with him before.

"Are you calm?" Commander Mars barked as soon as they were alone in Hendrex's office.

Hendrex continued to seethe for a moment before he allowed himself to relax and forced himself to refocus.

"I apologize for getting out of hand. That is not the way a member of the Ruling Council should handle disputes. No matter how worthy the opponent is of physical retribution."

Commander Mars smiled and shook his head.

"To be honest, it's nice knowing at least one of our leadership is good in a fight. I may not be allowed to speak my mind down there, but in all honesty, I don't believe you have done anything wrong. I, too, see what's happening here, and I am glad you at least know what needs to be done. I am in no position to offer much help, but I will do what I can to keep Donovan at your disposal. The human world will never be completely safe, but that doesn't mean we shouldn't prepare for a future in it," Commander Mars said.

Hendrex was taken aback by the show of support. It made him feel slightly less alone in his observations. He opened his mouth to speak when there was a flare of energy at the door. Commander Mars visibly stiffened. Adopting the gruff, authoritative posture he was known for before opening the door.

Two Security Force Officers stood outside; one spoke in a hushed tone to Commander Mars. When Commander Mars stepped aside and allowed the men to take hold of Hendrex's arms, he knew he was in serious trouble.

"What is going on?" Hendrex demanded.

"In light of your show of violence, the Ruling Council has agreed to suspend your authority as Ruling Four until after the trial," Commander Mars said.

Hendrex bit his tongue to keep from arguing. It wouldn't do any good. The Ruling Council had every right to suspend him, even if the charges against him were bogus. Instead, he chose the high road. He pulled his arms from the Officers' grasps.

"I will see myself to my accommodations. No escort needed."

He stalked out of the room before they could protest. He

wasn't surprised when they tagged along anyway. Now more than ever, it was important that Maclovis be brought to testify. If this wasn't cleared up soon, there was no telling how bad things would get for the people of Ceres and the Aura as a whole.

...

Violets and vases littered the room where Enora sat chatting with Farrah's mother while Farrah sipped cognac and looked out of sorts with the whole situation.

"Oh, I'm so excited about this! I've waited a long time to see my Van married off, and we surely need a reason to celebrate in Ceres," Donovan's mother gushed as she carefully packed away the already completed centerpieces.

Farrah's mother and Enora eagerly nodded in agreement while Farrah downed her glass and poured herself another. It was not a good look, and Rye wouldn't stand for Farrah making a fool of herself in front of her new mother-in-law. Even if Farrah herself didn't care. Disrayan made her way over to her best friend and plucked the glass from her hand.

"You made the decision to have a Binding Ceremony. You don't get to take the easy way out with the planning. Especially since you dragged me away from important work to be here," Disrayan snapped and handed Farrah a pair of pruning shears.

It probably wasn't the best idea to hand her such sharp weaponry with the glare Farrah shot her way, but Disrayan shrugged it off and continued to prune away the extra leaves and stems until the bushel in front of her fit perfectly in the small round bowls.

Despite all the mixed feelings Disrayan had about preparing for a Binding Ceremony, it was a welcome distraction from everything else going on.

47

"You think I wanted all of this?" Farrah snorted.

"No, but that's what you signed up for, so deal with it," Zazzie jumped in.

Disrayan smiled at Zazzie, who was in charge of cutting and tying the ribbon around the glass vases to finish off the look. The monotony of the tasks satisfied Disrayan's need for control and the familiar banter between her best friends eased her mind.

"Oh, cheer up. Only thirty more to go," Enora said, fishing out another vase to polish to perfection.

Farrah began to shake her head and stood up.

"Donovan has to have some sort of update on the case by now," she said, heading toward the door.

"And he will surely let you know tonight when this is done. Don't bother the man while he is working," Farrah's mother chastised.

The older woman gave Farrah a look that had the ordinarily hard-headed Farrah cowering back to her bean bag chair to prune flowers. Disrayan smiled at Farrah's mother, and the woman smiled back before a sad look crossed her face. Disrayan turned away, knowing exactly what the woman was thinking about. A similar moment occurred when Farrah was protesting during the preparation for Disrayan and Mack's Binding Ceremony.

A deep ache settled in Disrayan's chest as if it were just yesterday that she stood waiting in her dress for someone to tell her where the hell Mack was and why he was late. Instead, he had been gone. No one knew where he was for over a year, and when he did show back up, it wasn't to apologize or make amends with her. Sure, the reminder of her own almost Binding hurt, but not as much as she thought it would. Maybe time did heal all wounds.

Disrayan shook her head and pulled out her phone. Farrah shouldn't bother Donovan, but as a Magistrate, Disrayan had every right to. Before she could even finish typing out her message, a notification appeared. She was needed back in Ceres, Ruling Four had just been suspended from his duties and placed on house arrest for assaulting Ruling Three.

If her copper skin could pale, it would have. Instead, she took a deep calming breath and excused herself from the room. The sad look Farrah's mom gave her, and the way her friends avoided eye contact, told Disrayan they all assumed her flight was because of old memories. Honestly, it was better that way. None of the women needed any new drama at the moment.

Disrayan gave a quick wave as she headed out the door, careful not to seem in too much of a hurry as she made her way from Farrah's apartment to the nearby Gate to Ceres. Her friends weren't the only ones she needed to keep out of the loop. If any of the Aura saw the Magistrate bolting for the Gate it would only fuel the mass hysteria the whole incident had started in the first place.

"What happened?"

Donovan was in an angry stare off with his father when she arrived to make the necessary notes in the Book of the Ruling Council.

"He lost it, plain and simple. There was nothing more we could have done. Ruling Four is lucky this is only a suspension," the Commander said.

Donovan rubbed over his face, a sign of frustration Disrayan had only seen when he dealt with Farrah.

"This is not good," Donovan grumbled.

"No, it isn't," Disrayan made her presence known.

Both men turned to her, grim expressions on their faces.

"Magistrate, I've had the Book of the Ruling Council brought out for your mark," Commander Mars got straight to business.

She moved toward the massive tome, which already lay open on the commander's desk. The incident report, along with the Council's ruling against Ruling Four, were ready for her to review. She shook her head as she signed her name next to the damning paragraph. This would make her job that much harder. Hendrex benefitted from certain protections as an active member of the Ruling Council. Now, she would need to prove that not only was he acting with the best interest of the Aura, but that he was even fit to make such judgment.

"How's the Binding Ceremony prep going?" Donovan said, failing to lighten the mood in the room.

"Farrah is getting drunk to cope, but your mothers are happily planning and executing. How's the case going?"

Donovan frowned and sighed.

"As long as I have Farrah, I don't give a damn about flowers and guest lists. As far as the case, I wish I could say we were getting closer to the source. We've found one more monster house, but it was already empty. They know we are looking for them now, and they are adjusting accordingly."

Disrayan had hoped for better news, but today didn't seem like it was going to be that kind of day.

"Well, you should go save Farrah before she makes your evening a living hell," Disrayan suggested.

Donovan nodded and smiled before patting Disrayan on the back and heading out the door. Commander Mars looked like he was going to say something more but instead shook his head and closed the book.

"I can make sure this gets back to the Archives. I'm headed there anyway," Disrayan said.

She picked up the hefty tome before he could protest and hurried from his office. She was just outside of the Archives when she ran into Ruling Three. The weight of the tome added to the force of her momentum and knocked the older man over. He went sprawling to the ground, legs in the air, robes over his head. Disrayan couldn't help the smirk on her face before she offered a formal, if not a sincere, apology.

"I'm so sorry, Ruling Three." She nodded her head briefly.

He scoffed and fought off the Security Force Officers who tried to help him.

"You, young Magistrate, need to watch where you are going," he spat. His eyes glittered with anger.

Disrayan couldn't help but feel like his words were more of a threat than an admonishment. She turned her own glare upon the man.

"I offer the same advice, Ruling Three. With the instability of the moment, all of our safety deserves extra consideration."

With that said, Disrayan marched off toward the Archives. She could hear Ruling Three grumbling behind her, but didn't catch enough to make out what he said. Judging by the tone and the tense energy rolling from him, it wasn't anything good. Disrayan couldn't afford to be seen as biased, but that man rubbed her the wrong way.

Thinking of being rubbed, Disrayan's thoughts drifted to the other night with Mack. He rubbed her in so many different ways Disrayan barely knew which way was up. With a dreamy sigh, she put the Book of the Ruling Council back in its place. Out of the corner of her eye, she spotted something odd. One of the older texts was out of place. She pulled it from the shelf and was about to replace it when she stopped herself. It was a book of the old stories. One that should be in the restricted section, the few Archives only the Ruling Council and Commander of the Security Force had access to. The book fell open to the story of Maura. She had heard the myth countless times in oral retelling, but from the start, this one was different.

Disrayan read the opening paragraph twice, just to be sure she was translating it correctly. A chill ran up her spine. In the oral tradition, the story began with Maura already having amassed her power. Reigning terror amongst human and supernatural alike. This written story started much further back, when Maura was still human, a brutalized blood slave. Disrayan couldn't help but continue to read. She had no idea why, but she felt there was some connection to this telling of Maura and the current situation. It could hardly be a coincidence that this particular book was out of place.

Glancing around the room to make sure no one else was there to see, Disrayan continued reading. Occasionally, she glanced up again, unable to shake the feeling of being watched. She chalked it up to the fact she was doing something she knew she shouldn't but couldn't resist the temptation to see what all the secrecy was about.

By the end of the story, Disrayan was shaken and even more confused. The book was from the line of Commanders and ended with handwritten notes from Commander Mars himself. He apparently kept Maura's supposed ex-minions under surveillance. Their names weren't listed—only the numbers six, seven, eight, and finally a nine with a female symbol next to it.

What really struck fear into her was the evidence that Maura was still alive and possibly the mastermind behind the Aura disappearances. Disrayan pulled out her phone to message Farrah and Donovan about her discovery, then stopped. If Commander Mars knew about this already, why wouldn't he have mentioned it to Donovan? Donovan surely already knew about this, and if he didn't? No one would believe her mad tale. On top of that, she would be in even more trouble for having read the secrets of the Commanders without permission.

She bit her lip and scowled. This may be useful information or an entirely made up tale. A plant to distract her from the real issue. That opened up a whole other can of worms that Disrayan decided was of no use to dig into at the moment. No, it was best that she remain focused on getting Hendrex out of the trouble he found himself in. The Aura needed a stable governing body if they were going to survive whatever the fates had in store for them.

A slight breeze caught her attention, and Disrayan looked toward the door. No one was there, but the tent flap fluttered as if someone had just disturbed it. Her gut instinct had been right. She was being watched, but by who? The list of possible suspects was rather short. Commander Mars may be leading her to something, or it could Ruling Three wanting to discredit her in any way he could. Either option wasn't ideal. Disrayan slammed the book closed and hurriedly returned it to the spot she found it. She moved along the stacks to find the books she originally came to find and pulled them from the shelves. Farrah and Donovan would get the answers they needed as far as the Aura trafficking. It was up to Disrayan to figure out the mess with the Ruling Council.

Vision

It took Mack less time than the GPS estimated for him to arrive at the upscale rehab center. Still, it gave him enough time to shake off the dread in his heart and present his usual deadpan cheer for his friend. Mack parked in one of the visitor spots and got out of the vehicle. Since he'd been the one to check Shane in, Mack had to go inside to finalize checking him out. Even with showing up well past normal business hours, Mack knew he wouldn't be keeping anyone from their after-work plans. This particular facility catered to Vampires, as well as other high-profile clientele that necessitated a graveyard staff.

Mack cracked a smile at the term graveyard. How fitting for the swath of rich undead in residence. Mack walked into the main entrance. A tinkling of harmonic bells signaled the front desk that he arrived. Not that they didn't already know from the security guard at the front gate or the multitude of motion sensitive cameras along the long gravel drive. His nostrils filled with the heavy floral scent of the incense burning from every corner of the room. Another layer of security to mask the human scent and keep the shifters from sneaking in to gather intel from or about the residents. The soft chanting of Buddhist monks tickled his ears while jewel colored throws and large plush bean bags decorated the space. It was meant to be soothing, but only made Mack more unsettled. The faster he was able to get out of here, the better. Thankfully, the smiling man at the front desk was competent at his job.

After signing in as a visitor and confirming his purpose there, Mack was given a badge and guided to the office of Shane's therapist. The female Vampire smiled pleasantly at him, but it didn't reach her eyes. She studied him for a moment not saying a word. It had been the same when he brought Shane to the facility. Dr. Hartford knew he was different but still couldn't place exactly how. Mack smiled and took a seat across from her desk.

"Shane told me he's ready to come home," Mack started the conversation.

She blinked twice before taking a seat across from him.

"He thinks he is ready, but I feel he has a long way to go before he's in the clear of his addiction," she stated.

"So, your professional opinion is to have him stay?" Mack asked, and he saw a glimmer of something in the woman's eye.

Mack fought the urge to read the woman's energy. It was something he learned early in his investigating that he could do with relative ease. However, Vampire energy was different than humans, or even shifters. It was thick and tended to cling to you, influencing your own energy heavily. It was a feeling Mack didn't need when his body was already in protest.

"For what ails him, staying wouldn't do any good. You brought him in for substance abuse. You failed to mention his attachment to the human love he lost," she said.

Mack sighed and leaned back in the chair. Of course, he'd known Shane's feelings for Molly were very much his problem.

He'd hoped that some time away would help to clear Shane's mind of the guilt that drove him to his self-destructive state. Then again, Mack's situation with Disrayan was testament to the fact that distance didn't heal a broken heart.

"But his substance abuse is good to go?" Mack chose to focus on that issue first.

Shane's issues with Molly weren't as bad as when he left. Mack knew for a fact that Molly was just as excited for his return as Cat and the others.

"The root of his problem is not gone or forgotten, so there is always risk of relapse," Dr. Hartford stated.

"I assure you that I will be sure to check in frequently to keep him on the straight and narrow," Mack said.

He was getting antsy. He didn't like being under this shrewd woman's gaze. It was as if any minute she would guess what and who he was. His secret would be revealed, and he may end up locked in one of the rooms here. Not as a patient, but as an experiment. If there was one thing the Aura had correct about the modern world, it was that Vampires still weren't to be trusted with the knowledge of their existence. At least, not typical Vampires. Xander and Claude hadn't asked for confirmation, but after enlisting their help with the raid, Mack was certain they at least knew he wasn't just a human in the know.

"I would hope so. Shane is waiting in the courtyard. I will show you the way."

Dr. Hartford stood and pasted a smile on her face. Mack couldn't help his curiosity and allowed himself a peek at what was hidden behind those blinding pearly whites. What he met made his stomach turn once again. Her soul was as black as the depths of hell. Blacker even than the Aura traffickers he'd helped take down last week. The screams of a thousand lost souls echoed in his brain. She enjoyed the pain of others; her job as a therapist only fed part of her craving for misery. The rest was satisfied by dark deeds best left undiscovered. The darkness weighed heavily on his soul, even heavier were the traces of Aura energy he found.

Energy that wouldn't be there had she not fed from an Aura recently. Mack quickly stood to make his escape, but forced himself to slow his movements. It could be a coincidence. Maybe an Aura in need of easy cash had donated blood to one of their false blood banks. No need to alert her to his distrust any more than she already knew.

He straightened his posture, standing at his full height to show he was in no way intimidated by the smaller woman. Even though she was a Vampire, and he was clearly just a human. Dr. Hartford rounded her desk, and he followed her through the bare walled halls. Her short heels clicked along the wooden floors filling the silence between them. Mack thought Shane would be safe here, but now he wasn't so sure. Even if Shane wasn't as recovered as he claimed, Mack couldn't in good conscience leave him here now.

Dr. Hartford made a quick left into a large sitting room. It was also filled with jewel tones and heavy incense. The chanting monks sounded more ominous than soothing as the woman opened the glass doors that led to the lush garden outside. On the surface, this place appeared a relaxing haven of healing. The longer Mack was inside the gilded fortress, he was beginning to see it for what it was. A glorified castle of horrors.

At least it didn't take long for them to find Shane. He was sitting in front of a rose bush chatting with a petite blonde woman. Mack almost didn't recognize him. For as long as Mack had known Maura's Men, Shane had always been rail-thin and gaunt. Seeing him now, he had a better idea of what Maura had coveted in the man. Although still not as massive as the other two Vampires deemed Maura's Men, Shane's muscles wrapped in thick cords around his arms, and his chest was broad and defined beneath his thin cotton shirt.

Even his once scraggly and patchy beard had filled in with thick brown hair with hints of red that glinted in the fading sunlight. Even rarer still, the genuine smile that lit up his face with a healthy glow as he chatted excitedly with the woman next to him.

"Shane, your visitor has arrived," Dr. Hartford said, causing an abrupt silence to fall between the couple.

The blonde woman turned a sad smile toward Mack as Shane stood to greet him.

"Thank you!"

Shane embraced Mack in an enthusiastic hug. Mack hadn't been aware the man was a hugger. Then again, he had been turned around the time of what the humans called the 'love generation'. Mack hugged the man back, but pulled away as soon as he respectfully could.

"You ready to go?"

Mack, for one, was ready to leave. His skin still crawled from the energy he read from the doctor.

"Absolutely," Shane said with a reserved sigh.

"So soon!"

The blonde pixie stood from her perch on the low brick wall. She looked genuinely concerned at the idea of Shane leaving. Mack studied her energy and found nothing immediately troubling about the woman. Shane turned to his friend and pulled her into a hug. Mack stopped his reading. He didn't want to feel whatever the girl was feeling in that moment, but that didn't mean that he was okay with this friendship just yet. The traces of Aura energy within the Vampire female, as well as the doctor, confirmed this place was nowhere he needed to be. The odds of one bag of Aura blood finding its way into Vampire hands wasn't exactly condemning, but two was something to note. Especially given the revelation of Vampires trafficking young female Aura.

"Thank you for everything. I hope one day to see you again, but for now, I must return home," Shane said to the woman.

Mack studied Shane as he exchanged goodbyes and promises to stay in touch. Thankfully, Shane hadn't been a recipient of Aura blood. Once again, Maura's Men were proving to be less monstrous than those that had condemned them. However, there was a bit of a red flag in the swell of gratitude he felt. If he didn't know any better, he'd think Shane had formed more than just a friendship with the young woman. Part of him was relieved at the idea, but another knew Shane was destined to be with Molly. Further confirmation that Shane returning home was for the best. This woman and their relationship had the potential to destroy what little chance remained in Shane's relationship with Molly.

The sooner he and Molly reconciled, the sooner everyone else would refocus on the effort to rid the world of Maura once and for all. Only then could they all have the happy lives they had been deprived. Not just Xander, Claude, and Shane, but Mack as well. Once the threat of Maura was vanquished, he could start rebuilding the life he left behind. The life he envisioned with Disrayan, if she ever forgave him.

...

Ruling Three peered out the darkened windows of his town car. He hated being outside the Barrier, but this was business. For his plan to work, he needed a little extra push. The people of Ceres needed to fear the outside world again. Needed to doubt the other Ruling Council members. Ruling One and Two were already taken care of. The people no longer trusted them. Their advanced age and backward thinking made them easy targets.

No, it was Hendrex Andromeda who was the thorn in his side. The blip in his plan. He took a gamble revealing the information he knew about Ruling Four's secret investigations. Unfortunately, it looked to backfire.

Even his most loyal supporters didn't see the fault in his plan to allow more integration with the human world. That led Ruling Three here to a desperate and dangerous act. Relying on the saying, the enemy of my enemy is my friend, he'd brokered this contract long ago. He just never thought he'd have to cash in on the favor so soon.

With a sigh, Ruling Three got out of the car. The red brick mansion was massive to him. Way bigger than anything in Ceres. A grandeur that could only be achieved when space wasn't a premium. He stalked up the steps, and the grand wrought iron door swung open before he reached the landing. A pale young man dressed in a perfectly pressed suit gestured for him to enter.

"Master is awaiting you in the study," he said.

Ruling Three nodded and allowed the man to lead him down the hall. It turned out to be a grandiose library. Larger even than the Archives in Magelor. Plush leather furniture surrounded a blazing hearth, and the man of the hour sat behind an antique desk sipping a snifter of spirits.

"Seth, I'm surprised you requested a personal meeting. How trusting of you," Maximus said.

Ruling Three put on a brave face. He couldn't show weakness now, especially when he came to ask a favor. The agreement stood on the grounds that the main players remain anonymous, but these were desperate times.

"I came to apologize for the loss of your men. I had no knowledge of the raid, or I would have passed along the information sooner," Ruling Three said.

The Vampire smirked and shook his head.

"Apology not accepted or needed. You brokered our deal based on false information. Why should I trust you to live up to your end of the bargain any longer? I know enough now; I don't need you."

Ruling Three's blood ran cold. It had been a mistake to come alone.

The Vampire stopped glaring at Ruling Three, and his features softened until he was bent over with laughter.

"I'm sorry, you are just so easily read. No wonder the Aura are in such dire straits. They need the leadership of their true masters."

Ruling Three bristled at that idea. He may be callous enough to offer Auraless women to the Vampires, to feed their addictions, but Ceres itself was never in the bargain. As it was, the Vampire had no idea Ceres existed. He only knew that Ruling Three was influential in the small Aura community that resided in Langsmith.

"That's enough! I came here to make amends by providing you a guaranteed haul," Ruling Three snapped.

He was in no mood to be mocked. The Vampire straightened, anger flashing in his soulless gaze. In an instant, the Vampire was in his face.

"Raise your voice to me again, and you will be next on the auction block," he hissed.

Now it was Ruling Three's turn to smirk.

"I'd like to see you try. You have no idea my specialty. Anyway, this one won't be easy to catch, but she is powerful. More powerful than all of the others combined. I'll send word through the usual channels. Get this one, and I can promise you more."

Ruling Three didn't wait for an answer. He needed to get back to Ceres before the spell he cast on the gate guards wore off. The same spell he'd used on the poor soul he set up for the fall of the Barrier. No one could know the details of his plan. He touched his face where it was still sore from Ruling Four's fist. One obstacle was out of the way, and as soon as he got rid of that retched Magistrate, he could proceed toward his goals.

Pine

Fresh pine, that was the scent that greeted Jaquis as he climbed out of the Uber he'd taken to the middle of nowhere. It wasn't exactly nowhere, the entrance to the shifter compound was just down the dirt drive in front of him. A lone mailbox and a rusty looking gate were the only indication there was anything down the narrow winding path. His Uber's sedan wouldn't have been able to make the rest of the drive, even if Jaquis had been allowed to bring a human into shifter territory.

At least Jaq had worn his old Timbs because this was about to be a hike. He barely got a few feet onto the path before he caught movement from the corner of his eye. Despite being invited to the property, Jaq threw off a cautioning wave of energy at the circling shifter. He wouldn't be foolish enough to actually attack a shifter on shifter land, but Jaq would definitely defend himself if necessary.

There was more movement to his left before a young man emerged from the brush wearing nothing but a pair of basketball shorts.

"Follow me," the kid said and marched away from the main path.

Jaq shook his head before following. He should have prepared for this. Shifters were notoriously secretive. He may have been invited to the property, but that didn't mean he would be handed the knowledge of their exact location. Even if he happened to be friends with the pack leader. A bit of info he hadn't shared when Mack asked to set up a meet. Jaq had been surprised that Tyr called him, just after he hung up with Mack, requesting a meet all on his own. The perfect opportunity to feel out if his friend would be open to meet with the others. A hard sell, but Jaq was sure he could do it.

He followed the boy off the main path, thankful there seemed to be a smaller, less traveled path that they were following. It was a short and silent walk through the wooded area until the path opened to a small clearing. Jaq recognized Tyr, the pack leader, standing in the middle of the clearing. He did not recognize the young girl who was poised beside him in a loose attack stance. Her chest heaving, brow dripping sweat from exertion. Several other teens stood around watching intensely.

Tyr smiled at Jaq before nodding at the young girl.

"Enough training for today."

The girl frowned at Jaq before taking off into the woods, followed by the others and the boy who led Jaq to the clearing.

"What's with all the cloak and dagger?"

Jaq took a seat on one of the logs the teens had vacated.

Tyr grabbed a discarded t-shirt and pulled it over his head.

"There's something not right about the situation with Ceres."

"Ceres?"

Jaq decided it best to keep up the charade of ignorance

about the rumored Aura Sanctuary. Tyr probably knew more about what was going on inside Ceres than he did.

Tyr chuckled and shook his head.

"Hypothetically, if the Great Sanctuary did exist. If the Barrier that kept it hidden somehow weakened. What would that mean for the Aura population within?"

Jaq sighed, debating how much he should let on. It was common knowledge amongst the supernatural in Langsmith that Jaq was an Aura Liberationist. The last pack leader had sent many a threat his way about encouraging a similar movement amongst the shifter population. Tyr however, had always been friendly with Jaq. He didn't want to burn any bridges that he may need to cross if things in Ceres were as dire as Tyr and Mack's urgent calls let on.

"I don't deal in hypotheticals, but if I did, I'd say the only indicator to that would be time. If there is a sudden increase of Aura in the area, there may be reason for concern."

"Would I be able to count on you to notify me if you noticed anything strange? Perhaps, in exchange for information involving the Vampires' sudden interest in a certain factory?"

Jaq saw his opening then and smiled.

"Actually, I did have a favor to ask. My cousin would like to have a private meeting with you about the state of everything."

Tyr raised a brow and shook his head.

"You know I don't do secret dealings."

"All you do is secret dealings," Jaq laughed and swung his arm around to make a point.

"Fine, I'll bite as long as you can be more specific about

what he would like to discuss."

"Keep those fangs to yourself, wolf man. It's just a friendly chat amongst concerned parties in the Langsmith area. If anything, you will be getting firsthand information from sources you never imagined possible."

Jaq watched as Tyr considered him. The man's nose twitched as he sniffed the air before he shook his head.

"I may regret this later, but fine. I'll take you back to the city. I've got some errands to run anyway."

"Thanks, I don't think I could get my Uber back here anyway."

"You took an Uber? Pissed off your lady friend, did you?"

"Keep your nose out of my love life," Jaq spat.

"Get you a solid mate, man. It'll change your life," Tyr laughed and climbed into his truck.

Listed

Mack wished he could stay in bed with Rye all night. To be there when she woke up, make her breakfast, and have the talk they both so desperately needed to have, but it would have to wait. He was already late for his shift at the Club, and with Maura's increased activity as of late, he couldn't bail. She looked so peaceful in her sleep, no worry lines creased the outer corners of her eyes and mouth, no tense set to her shoulders or jaw. She lay beside him with a soft smile and a healthy after sex glow to her cheeks and body.

Mack kissed her lips and then her forehead before sliding out of the bed. He hoped she wouldn't be pissed to find him gone in the morning, but Mack was also pretty sure she might be relieved. Despite knowing she still cared for him, still craved his body, no one knew better than Mack how dauntless she could be once she set her mind to something. Right now, her mind was set on keeping her feelings for Mack at bay. Something he wasn't sure he wanted to change given their circumstances. It was the catch twenty-two of their current situation. He loved her and wanted to protect her at all costs. Even if that meant being the asshole to break her heart so he could save her and the rest of the world from the threat of Maura's evil plans.

He had no idea when the threat of Maura would be neutralized, and by then, who's to say Disrayan wouldn't have moved on to someone else. Someone less dangerous and duty bound as he. Mack followed the trail of his clothing back to the living room, getting dressed along the way. His phone buzzed in his pocket as soon as he pulled on his pants.

He didn't recognize the number and almost didn't answer it, but when they called a second time as he was gently closing Rye's front door behind him, Mack answered.

"Yes," he said.

"Hey, It's Jaq. I just got word from my source. The meeting is a go," Jaq said.

"Great. Is this a new number, or are you just being careful about your contacts?" Mack asked.

"You can never be too careful. Speaking of which, I gotta go."

Jaq didn't wait for Mack to reply before hanging up. With a shake of his head, Mack dialed Donovan's number. Donovan answered on the first ring.

"Did you set up the meeting?"

Of course, Donovan wouldn't beat around the bush.

"Yeah, it's done. I'll send you more details when I have them."

"Good."

Donovan, too, wasted no time with pleasantries and hung up.

Two key players down, one to go.

Mack knew this meeting was necessary, but he also knew he was taking a big risk in setting this all up. The issue of the Vampires trafficking Aura was certainly a problem, and may also help with figuring out just how powerful their enemies were or would become. Mack just wanted the world to be safe. He knew Ceres wasn't able to sustain the entire Aura population, and that meant more needed to be done to ensure their safety outside of the Sanctuary. Number one was getting rid of Maura for good, and number two was ensuring the Aura didn't become subjected to other horrors by the Vampires. It was a tall order, but like Disrayan, Mack could be just as stubborn with his goals.

...

Disrayan sat at the other end of the bar. The last place she wanted to be was in the Vampire hang out, Club Obelisk, but it was the only place that she knew would get Mack's attention and avoid getting distracted.

Yeah, because you wouldn't have to be here if you wouldn't have fallen into bed with him earlier.

Her body still ached from the exertion of their pleasure. If it hadn't been for the black cat mewling loudly by her window, Disrayan may not have woken up in time to even catch Mack at work. A part of her was still pissed he had snuck out, even knowing it was to go to work. Likewise, she was here on business. To deliver the official summons of the Ruling Council personally. To ensure he got it, since he hadn't responded to the first one. It wasn't a social call. Ruling Four needed Mack to testify, so they could put this whole mess behind them.

"You're far from home," a familiar voice said.

Disrayan turned to see Claude, one of the Vampires that helped with saving the women a few days ago. She smiled at him in an attempt to mask her unease.

"I came to see Mack," she said.

The Vampire smiled, careful not to reveal his fangs. He ran a hand through his sandy blond hair before leaning against the bar next to her. His eyes never met hers, just continued to scan the crowd.

"I noticed you two had some history. I'm not going to pry, but Mack has become a trusted friend. I don't wish to see him unhappy," Claude said.

"Is that supposed to be a threat?" Disrayan asked.

"Not from me, but you see the redhead at VIP? She might not take kindly to you messing with her favorite employee. Especially, while he's at work. Trust me when I say you do not want to get on her bad side," he said.

Disrayan let her eyes travel to the huddle of Vampires on the roped-off platform. A stunning red-haired woman stood surveying the masses below. Her body language reeked of power and authority. The woman made eye contact with Mack, and they both smiled at each other. A knot of jealousy formed in Disrayan's stomach, and she looked away.

"I'm not here on a personal matter. If it weren't time sensitive, I wouldn't be here at all."

"I don't blame you. It's not exactly safe for your kind around here."

"What do you mean my kind?"

Disrayan was suddenly suspicious of the Vampire. Claude had seemed nice enough during the mission. He'd been quite charming actually, but today, he was anything but. His posture was aggressive, and his words, well, he wasn't exactly being welcoming. Maybe it was the vibe of the club.

"Young, beautiful women," he said plainly before pushing

away from the bar.

His eyes landed on something he obviously didn't like. Claude's energy spiked with a possessive rage. Disrayan watched as the crowd parted in his wake, and the other Vampires went on red alert. He stopped in front of the mousey brunette with a funky scarf tied around her neck. She looked pissed at the human male in front of her, but before the Vampire could reach the man, she stood between the two.

Disrayan watched amused as the woman faced off with the massive Vampire and made him look like a puppy who'd just misbehaved. When Claude grabbed the woman and kissed her like they were at home in a bedroom, instead of in a public place, Disrayan shook her head. Of course, he'd been on edge. The woman was his mate, and she worked in a nightclub. Vampire males were notoriously possessive, especially of their female mates. It was a wonder he allowed her to work outside the home at all.

"Can I get you a drink?"

Disrayan turned and faced Mack. He didn't look at all pleased she was at his place of work. Granted, she, at least, expected him to be happy to see her after screwing her senseless a few hours ago.

"No, actually, I came here on business," Disrayan said, and pulled the short missive from where it was tucked in her bra.

In the tight, black dress she wore, there really hadn't been any other place for it. She could have worn something better suited to her task, but when she saw the dress hanging forgotten in her closet, she changed at the last minute. She'd hoped Mack would recognize it. It was the dress she would have worn to their final courtship dinner. The dress she'd laid out on their bed before joining Mack for an intimate shower. The same dress he'd helped her into before his phone rang. A call she told him to ignore, but he hadn't. Whatever was said on the other end had been more important to him than their future together.

"Everything is business with you, Rye," Mack said, snatching the paper from her hand.

Disrayan chose not to comment on his rude behavior, or his use of her nickname. It was an extra twist to the knife he left in her heart. Her hand curled into a fist as she fought the stinging words that sat at the tip of her tongue. Here and now wasn't the time or place to make a scene. Mack tore open the official seal of the Ruling Council and read the three lines carefully scrawled by Ruling One herself.

"I've been asked to bring you in as soon as possible," Disrayan said.

"You? Why? I thought my lack of response was answer enough the first time. Did they think you had some sort of clout with me because..." He left the sentence hanging between them.

"No, they just didn't think sending a Security Force Officer would give the right impression. You are not under investigation. It's Ruling Four that needs your help," Disrayan said plainly.

"Well, if Hendrex is that hard up, he can come to me himself. I don't have time for the Ruling Council's bullshit. I have more important things to attend to," Mack spat and started to walk away to assist the customers lining up to be served.

"Like what? Tending to these Vampire scum?" Disrayan snapped, and Mack glared at her.

His stare was ice, but it wasn't his eyes that worried her. Several Vampires nearby heard her angry comment and turned their beady eyes in her direction. She didn't need this scrutiny. Mack stalked around the counter and grabbed her arm. He didn't say a word until they were out of the club and on the street, away from the line of people waiting to get in.

"You don't get to judge my chosen profession. You, for sure, don't get to judge these people. Check your hate and your privilege before you end up with a reckoning that neither of us will like," he hissed.

Disrayan pulled her arm from his grasp.

"Says the man who walked away from everything because he couldn't handle just how good his life truly was," she sneered.

"The only good in my life was you, and that's what hurt the most. Knowing I was never anything but a fucking box for you to check in your quest for relevance. Tell your Ruling Council they can wipe their asses with this missive, and you stay the hell away from this place," Mack said, and he stormed back into the club before Disrayan could reply.

She stood there for several minutes, so angry she didn't notice the cold at first. Even as her breath heaved great clouds of fog in front of her. Just staring at the entrance to the club that he disappeared into. Disrayan hated how he knew just what to say and do to get under her skin. She shouldn't care this much. Not anymore. He obviously thought terrible things about her, and if there was one thing she knew about Mack, once his mind was made up about someone, there was no going back.

The cold finally began to seep into her consciousness, but as soon as it registered, a large black coat was draped over her shoulders.

"You really shouldn't be out here like this," a familiar voice said.

Disrayan turned to see Alexander, the other Vampire from that night.

"I know, I was just leaving."

Disrayan shrugged out of his coat and handed it back to him. She took off down the street before he could offer her any more comfort. Disrayan never in a million years thought she would be that comfortable around a Vampire. Once again, Mack was turning her world upside down.

Clandestine

Mack resisted the urge to look at his watch. Donovan had said he was on his way, but here Mack was, waiting in a dark fucking alley well past the time they specified to meet. He caught the flare of Donovan's energy just before he was about to bail on the man and go to the meeting alone. Jaq would be pissed about the wasted favor, but Mack could handle his cousin.

"Sorry, I had a hard time shaking Farrah."

Mack looked over the large Security Force Officer and shook his head. Sex energy was all over the man.

"Look, I'm not the one who's going to throw a fit. Do you know how hard it is to get a meeting with Tyr Greywulf?"

Donovan snorted and rolled his eyes.

"Nosy shifter is probably dying for this meeting."

"Shelve the attitude, and let's go before Farrah tracks your ass."

"Don't get snippy with me. I can still haul your ass back to Ceres for proper justice."

"You don't have anything on me, otherwise you'd have done it a long time ago. I'm not exactly hiding."

Mack headed down the alley toward the blue door that would lead them to the meeting place. An abandoned office building not far from the warehouse district.

"Where is this meeting anyway?"

"If I told you, it wouldn't be a secret meeting. Also, Jaq is going to be there, so keep your eyes on the prize. We need answers about the Vampire involvement with the missing Aura."

Donovan flared with anger.

"You think I would risk this opportunity over Jaq?"

"If your flaring is any indication, hell yeah. Remember, I'm only here as a courtesy. What we get out of this meeting is entirely up to you."

Mack waited for Donovan to reel himself in before continuing on his path. Farrah was definitely rubbing off on Donovan. The man's ability to control himself was definitely lacking now that he was shacked up with Mack's cousin. He just hoped Donovan didn't throw a fit once he saw Xander there as well. It was important that all sides were represented in this case. More was at stake than just the fate of these Aura women. If Maura was involved in any way? That could spell disaster for all supernatural.

...

Tyr laughed at the off-color jokes Jaquis Andromeda made at the old white Vampire's expense. Xander didn't look all that pleased, but to his credit, he at least attempted to crack a smile.

"I will have to share that one with my mate. She enjoys making petty jokes about my paleness."

"You sure about that? Cat will want to know where you learned it, and I know you don't want to open that can of worms."

Mack Andromeda stepped out of the shadows, followed by Donovan Mars. Tyr had done his research on all the men he'd come to meet today. Even pulled old archives to ensure it was safe to come alone for this meeting. The old Vampire chuckled before nodding.

"Thank you, Mack. I don't wish to keep secrets from my mate, but I also don't want her to become involved in whatever this is."

"Consider it the supernatural Avengers. The X-Men, if you will," Jaq supplied.

Mack snorted, and Tyr shook his head while Donovan and Xander stared at each other confused.

"It's a human show about human mutants that fight other human mutants. Funny that you should bring that up, Jaq, considering The Resistance is basically the bad guy in that scenario," Tyr said.

Jaq shrugged.

"Depends on how you look at it."

"Enough of this. Most of us have mates waiting on us to return, so can we get down to business?" Donovan said, and pulled up a chair.

"To defeat the Huns?"

The room turned to stare at Xander, who now had a huge grin on his face.

"My mate has a soft spot for Disney films," he said after a moment.

The men in the room all laughed.

"Seriously, though, I'm probably the least in the loop, so fill me in," Jaq said.

Tyr exchanged looks with Donovan. Not sure if he should speak first or not. It was probably best if he stayed silent for now. He was unsure of what exactly this meeting was about as well. Was he finally going to get answers about Ceres? Were they here to feed him half-truths to throw him off their trail? The Gate had reopened, but there was something fishy going on about the whole situation.

"A little over a week ago, we took down a blood slave house. They were keeping Aura women," Mack said.

Tyr sat up at that. He'd been aware that something major had happened among the rogue Vamps. Hell, he even knew a little about their blood slave racket. He, himself, had sent parties to save young shifters from their clutches. Although, shifters were used in illegal fighting rings, instead of for their blood. Human blood slaves were a given for the Vampire community. Even though drinking from the source was outlawed by civilized vamps, rogues did their own thing.

"You think they've found a way to target the Aura?"

"Not think, we know. Over half the women saved were Aura. Weak to nearly Auraless, but of the Aura community all the same. We need your help in tracking down the ring leader. The Aura population is small and weak as it is without them picking off our youth," Donovan said.

"On that, we can agree," Jaq said.

Tyr looked between the two men.

"Why don't you just wrangle everyone together in Ceres?"

Donovan glared at Tyr.

"Ceres is a myth."

Tyr smirked and shook his head.

"You do know who you are talking to here. I have eyes and ears all over town. That giant magical gate at your factory is not as big a secret as you think."

"It's a portal, but it does not lead to Ceres. Like I said, Ceres is a myth. That Gate, as you call it, is simply an easier way to travel."

Tyr could scent the man's lie, but didn't want to push his luck. He needed to gain their trust if he was ever going to get the information he craved. Besides, having a powerful Aura on his side could come in handy in a number of ways. Shifters, as the spies of the supernatural world, had many enemies. The more powerful his allies, the safer the Langsmith Pack would remain.

"Evacuate the Langsmith area until the threat is gone."

"I was thinking we could team up in the investigation. Tyr, you have the information, Jaq has access, Donovan has his abilities and detective skills, and Xander has the muscle," Mack said.

Tyr eyed the man. He knew Mack was Aura, but he didn't scent the way the others did. The man's energy made the hair on Tyr's body stand on end. Almost the same way it did when Vampires were near. Something about the undead triggered the protectiveness of his beast.

"I don't give information for free, and it's against pack rules to interfere in inter species conflicts."

Even as he said the words, Tyr knew he would end up breaking those rules. Everything about this situation rubbed him the wrong way. The intel Sarah provided about the power-ful Aura sneaking around with Vampires, the trouble with the gate, and now learning Vampires were involved with missing Aura in the Langsmith area. That didn't bode well for any of the supernatural. There was a delicate balance to be maintained amongst the communities, otherwise things would surely implode.

"So, you aren't going to help?" Xander spoke this time. A harsh set to his mouth.

Tyr made a point of looking every man in the eye.

"Oh, I'll help, but this has to remain between us in this room. I don't like where this is looking to go. Langsmith has a balance that must be kept."

Xander and Donovan nodded in agreement.

"I guess we really are the super friends," Mack said, and Jaq shook his head.

"X-Men, we are the X-Men."

"Fuck the childish names. Let's see what we can dig up in a week, and we'll meet back here same time." Tyr didn't wait for their reply before he got up and left.

His mind raced with all the possibilities. One thing was for sure. He was going to need back up. The connections he made so far weren't boding well for the situation as a whole. To quote Shakespeare, "there was something rotten in Denmark," and it was his job to make sure his pack was covered when things went south. Tyr's phone buzzed in his pocket. He pulled it out, not surprised to see his mate Sequoia's face on the screen. Even twisted in a scowl, she was the most beautiful she-wolf.

"My dearest love, I am on my way home."

"Your dearest love, huh?"

Her frown softened into a smile before she tilted the phone

down her body, showing off the red lace lingerie set he'd left out on the bed for her. His cock jumped in his pants, and his wolf growled with approval. When the camera came back to her face, the smile was gone and she flicked him off before the screen went dark. With a shake of his head, Tyr shifted into his wolf and took off at a dead sprint.

...

Mack watched as Tyr shifted and ran into the dark. He hadn't meant to eavesdrop, but hearing the shifter and his mate reminded him so much of how he and Rye used to be.

Way to screw yourself over again.

Mack's inner voice had no pity for him. He had been a complete and total ass to Disrayan the other night. He could try to justify it all he wanted as protecting his undercover identity, and protecting her from the Vampire world he was immersed in. It didn't matter, he'd gone too far, and now would have nearly zero chance of her ever letting him back in.

"You look like you could use a drink," Jaq said, startling Mack.

"You just had to sneak up on me like that?"

Jaq laughed and clapped Mack on the shoulder.

"I have quite the track record with being in the doghouse with the ladies. I can offer some pointers to get back into Disrayan's good graces."

Mack sighed and shook his head.

"I think I'll pass on relationship advice from you, but I'll take the drink anyway."

Jaq and Mack headed toward the nearest bar. They could have gone drinking at Club Obelisk, since it was nearby, but both preferred the anonymity of a human bar for personal talks. Once at the bar, they grabbed a beer and found a table at the back away from the small crowd of regulars.

"Thank you for getting Tyr on board with this. I know it's a stretch to think this partnership between the supernaturals will last, but I feel like this is a start," Mack said.

Jaq took a swig of beer and shook his head.

"I'm not worried about this shaky alliance, I'm more worried about the issues making it necessary. I'm a rebel, but I'm not blind to the facts. Most Vampires are still not cool with the Aura, and I know the older generation has memories of the life before the Aura went into hiding. I realize they are still a threat."

"Like you said, not all of them are a threat. Xander, Shane, Claude. They are willing to help. They've endured their own form of persecution to know that it doesn't benefit anyone in the long run."

"Yeah, speaking of your 'friends,' how is it that you became so chummy with Maura's Men?"

Mack tensed.

"You know, the whole Maura thing is a myth."

Jaq smirked.

"Even if it is, those dudes have some serious dark energy about them. I've noticed how other Vampires steer clear."

Frustrated with the current conversation, Mack gulped down the rest of his beer and stood.

"Thanks for the beer, Jaq. You be careful out there with your little rebellion."

With that, he strode out of the bar. He could hear Jaq's

laughter behind him. Normally, Mack could have played it cool, but not tonight. His mind wasn't in the game like it should be. He wandered the streets of downtown, letting the brisk air help with his focus. He tentatively opened himself up to energy around him. Happy couples out on dates, local teens traipsing around without a care in the world. Under it all, though, was a darkness so bleak and evil that it clung to Mack's energy like sludge, feeding off it. Leeching the very essence of his being. Mack reeled his energy back in.

He surveyed the crowd around him, not seeing anyone in particular that stuck out, but he still couldn't help the knowing feeling in his gut that something wasn't right. His eyes went to the front of Club Obelisk, and he decided he should stop playing around and maybe do something useful. As soon as he stepped inside, his nerves were set at ease.

The familiarity and routine were exactly what he needed. Maybe by the end of the night he'd have the perfect plan to at least apologize to Disrayan. Mack was settling in behind the bar when he felt a shift in the energy around the club. It wasn't the two Vampires posturing over a young woman in the VIP section, either. The bouncers had that handled. No, this was a distress signal, a very intense distress signal from a very powerful Aura.

Mack was not about to let any Aura come to harm while he was around at Club Obelisk. Especially, with the trafficking ring now known to him. He rushed toward the energy. He spotted Shane and his blonde friend from the rehab facility walk around the corner. He wanted to think about what that meant or how that was even possible, but his priority was the Aura in trouble. A light like a spotlight flashed from inside the alley. He ran around the building only to find himself blinded by bright white light. He skidded to a halt, shielding his eyes until he could build a thick enough barrier with his own energy.

His void latched on to the power source like a moth to a

flame. He made his way toward the bright center of the energy source. Using more and more of his ability to shield himself from the increasingly intense energy. It rippled and thrashed at him violently, unrestrained. Mack had never experienced anything like this before. He'd never been able to fully unleash his energy with anyone, not even Disrayan, without fear of draining the life out of them.

He had to know who was at the center of this. He kept moving forward and paused when his vision finally cleared. He found Molly curled in a ball, eyes ablaze. Fiery red curls dancing like flames around her head. She looked absolutely pissed, eyes trained in the direction he'd seen Shane and his friend head. Shaking his head, he wrapped his arms around her and let his energy siphon from hers until she collapsed into his arms.

Almost as soon as she lost consciousness, Mack became aware of two Aura moving closer to their location. Of course, with a flare that size and that long, the Security Force would definitely come to investigate. Even with the Gate situation, or rather, especially because of the Gate situation, they would be on even more alert for breaches in secrecy. The Security Force was already up his butt about working at the club, and now with this flare, it only made things more complicated.

Mack hefted Molly and hustled her to his car. When she woke up, he would need to have a talk with her about controlling her emotions. Now wasn't the time to bring up that she was Aura, he would wait until she asked him directly. He wasn't sure how she would handle the news of being an Auraless. He didn't know much about her background, but maybe she already knew. He would have to wait and see. In the meantime, he could buy some time with the Security Force for her and help with the Shane situation. Nothing could have set Molly off like that unless it was close to her heart. Seeing Shane with someone else after everything they had been through; Mack could relate.

He couldn't afford to lose his shit like that no more than Molly could. As soon as he got Molly home and made sure she was all right, he would see Rye right away. He couldn't let this rift lay between them for much longer. He was an asshole, and he needed to find a flower shop that was open late.

Wake

Disrayan blinked twice to make sure she wasn't seeing things. Mack was indeed standing in her doorway with a bouquet of roses and an apologetic look on his face.

"What are you doing here?" She asked the obvious.

"What does it look like?" Mack invited himself inside.

Disrayan still held the door open. She wouldn't close it until she was sure of his motives. The last month had been a crazy emotional upheaval, and she didn't trust her judgment. Didn't trust that he was actually here to make amends and not to say a permanent goodbye.

"Thank you for the flowers, but I don't have time for whatever games you intend on playing."

"I'm not here to play games. I am here to apologize for earlier. I was rude to you, and I wanted you to know I wasn't trying to be hurtful."

Disrayan snorted and gestured toward the door she still

held open.

"Apology not accepted. Unless you came here to tell me you are willing to testify for your brother, you may see yourself out."

She didn't wait for him to move. She left the door ajar and stalked into her bedroom. It was late, and tomorrow was going to be yet another long day at the Archives. Maybe she could convince the Ruling Council to let her borrow a few tomes. It was a long shot, but traveling through the Gate so much was doing a number on her physically. Each crossing felt like she lost a piece of herself, and often meant losing anything she dared to eat beforehand.

"Rye," Mack called.

She felt his energy flare, calling to her, reaching out to connect in a way they hadn't in a long time. She refused to acknowledge it, to acknowledge him. Even if she wanted things to return to how they were before, he would have to do more than show up unannounced with flowers she didn't even have a vase for.

Lifting the covers on her bed, Disrayan heard the front door close with a not so subtle thump. She sighed and rolled her eyes.

"Forget you too, Mack," she muttered.

Maclovis could be angry all he wanted. She, personally, had had enough of his attitude. He was the one who left, he was the one who turned his back on her and on everything she once thought he stood for. He had no right to be angry at anyone or anything but himself.

...

When Rye ignored his flare of energy, Mack thought about

leaving. The door was wide open. All it would take was two small steps. He should leave. Disrayan obviously didn't want his apology, and he couldn't blame her. He hurt her when he left the first time. He hurt her again at Club Obelisk. In all honesty, if it weren't for his chat with Molly tonight, he probably would have let her be.

Seeing how distraught Molly had become over the idea of Shane moving on was something Mack could relate to, but the consequences were too much for him to allow. If Mack hadn't been there, Molly would have exposed herself as an Aura and possibly killed Shane and his friend in the process. Mack didn't want that for himself, or Disrayan. As much as he could try and pretend it wouldn't gut him to see her move on with someone else. Just the thought made his blood boil and his heart sink so far into the void of his energy that it took everything for him to hold it together.

With his hand still poised on the knob, Mack shook out his shoulders. His body still processing the massive energy intake from Molly's little meltdown. He felt like a hypocrite. Urging Molly to let Shane come to her in his own time, and yet, here he was forcing himself back into Disrayan's path. Knowing full well he couldn't give her what they both wanted. He wasn't sure he deserved her forgiveness. Especially when he couldn't offer her the truth.

"Don't be a wuss, Mack." With a shake of his head, his decision was made.

There would be no backing down, no backing away. Disrayan needed to know how he felt in no uncertain terms. If there was anything he'd learned from his undercover position monitoring Maura's Men, it was that love really did overcome even the most outrageous of obstacles.

Mack closed the front door before marching down the hall to Disrayan's room. She was already curled up in bed, her breathing soft and even. He quietly undressed and slid under the covers.

"I thought you left," she whispered.

"To be honest, I thought about it."

Her face twisted into a scowl before she tried to turn away, but Mack wrapped his arms around her, holding her too close for her to move. Her eyes locked with his, penetrating, searching. Mack felt raw and exposed. He fought the urge to avert his own gaze, instead, choosing to lean forward and press a soft kiss on the tip of her nose.

"Don't," she hissed.

Mack didn't listen. He kissed her cheeks, and then her chin. It was a game they used to play. He would kiss her everywhere but her mouth, breasts, and core. Giving himself space to maneuver, he trailed kisses along her neck and collarbone, the tops of her shoulders. Mack paid special attention to the crooks of her elbows and knees.

He didn't let his mouth do all the work. His hands traveled the planes of her body, reaching beneath her nightgown to trace the curve of her hips and ass. Mack tickled her inner thighs before switching to playful nips and licks. Disrayan writhed beneath him. Her hands gripped his head to guide him to the places she wanted him. He smiled as she tried to cheat and guide him directly to her dripping core. He parted her lips with his fingers, releasing the musky bouquet of her arousal.

Her muscles contracted, eager for his touch. Pulsing rhythmically and glimmering like the inside of a perfectly ripe peach. As much as he enjoyed teasing, the sight made him hunger for more. He traced the inside of her lips with his tongue, making a soft quick circle around her pulsating core before flattening his tongue to apply even pressure against her engorged clit.

"Mack!"

She gripped his shoulders, nails biting into his skin as her hips began to move. Sliding herself along his tongue, coating Mack's face with her juices as her body took what it needed. Mack allowed her a moment of weakness before pulling away. Her nails left stinging trails along the way.

"Easy, love, not yet."

"Don't call me love."

Mack flipped her onto her stomach and laid on top of her. Grabbing her arms, he placed them above her head.

"I'll call you whatever I got damn please," he growled in her ear.

Her body shivered with excitement. Mack pulled her night-gown up and over her head, using it to bind her wrists. He was taking a risk here. Normally, Disrayan preferred to dominate in the bedroom, as with every other aspect of her life. He straddled her now naked body. His dick strained against the cotton of his briefs. Rubbing his hand along her slit, he waited until she was purring beneath him before reaching into her night-stand and finding the slick glass dildo he knew she kept there.

So many things had changed about his beloved, and yet, that only made him love her more. He held the phallis in his hand, letting it warm in his grasp before teasing her with shallow penetrations. She pushed up on her knees a little, giving him a better angle, not just for the toy, but for viewing, as well. He couldn't resist leaning over and taking a bite of her plump cheeks as he penetrated her with the toy.

He soothed the bite with his free hand before licking his thumb and drawing lazy circles around the dark pucker of her asshole.

"I've dreamt of taking you here, ever since the night of the monster house," he breathed.

He pressed his thumb against her. She was still tight, but he was able to slide the tip of his digit in. He felt her clench hard against him, a keening moan escaping her. His other hand coated with more arousal. She was literally dripping at this point. Mack took his time, alternating rubbing and penetrating her behind; first, with his thumb, then with two fingers, then three. She relaxed into his ministrations. Pressing into his hand as much as he pressed his fingers into her. When he felt she was stretched enough to take it, Mack moved the glass dildo from her pussy and slid it into her ass.

He smirked as the clear glass gave him an inside view of her pink flesh. He played with her clit, watching with amazement at how her inner muscles clenched and rippled on the peak of orgasm.

"Oh! Oh! YES!"

The spasms intensified, Disrayan's body shook beneath his, and then the dildo was pushed from her body. It was the hottest thing he'd ever seen. He flipped Disrayan over and descended upon her. He kissed her. She moaned weakly, her body still quaking with the aftershocks of her orgasm.

"That, my love, was just the beginning," Mack said.

...

Gasping in shock, Disrayan woke to thick fingers penetrating her. Soft, butterfly kisses trailed down her spine and over her cheeks before she felt the rasp of Mack's short hair against her inner thigh. She missed the soft feel of his locks. Missed wrapping her hands in them as he worked her into a frenzy with his tongue. She reached down, pressing him further into her mound. She was being greedy, but Mack wouldn't mind.

When they'd been together, he'd enjoyed her eagerness

in bed. Nothing was taboo as long as it felt good. He knew exactly how she liked to be eaten. Gentle teasing forays over her sensitive clit while he stretched her. First with one finger, then two, until his entire fist rested inside of her. Disrayan gripped his shoulders as he suckled her hard. Her body exploded with sensation, only for it to be siphoned away in an instant.

"Damn you," she cursed.

"Not yet, Rye. I want my dick in you before you let go," he muttered.

His words muffled as she pressed her hips against his thick lips.

"Then, fuck me already," she demanded.

Mack slid back up her body, his fist still firmly embedded in her. He channeled the energy of her orgasm to the pucker of her ass. The trickle of pleasure he allowed easing the entry of his long, thick manhood. He buried himself deep, allowing her to adjust to the fullness. She wiggled against him, urging him to move. To ease the aching need for release. Instead, he toyed with her more.

"Your ass seems to welcome me just fine. Why can't you?"

Disrayan sighed, her arousal tempered by the reminder that this wasn't like the past. They weren't the happily courting couple on the eve of their Binding Ceremony.

"You left me, and after tonight, I'm sure you plan to do so again."

She squeezed her inner muscles in a rolling pattern. Stimulating his shaft and giving herself something to enjoy. She fed him more of her energy, as much as she could without setting off alarms at the Energy Monitoring System. The Gate may be closed, but that didn't mean the Security Force had stopped monitoring the human world for unauthorized energy use. If there was one thing that really got to Mack, it was energy play. In the past, they would spend hours mingling their energy, seeing what sensations they could bring out of one another.

Mack may be a powerful Aura in his own right, but Disrayan more than matched him. She may not have been born into a powerful family, but she knew her energy. The only person who knew the extent of what she could do was Mack. He was the only person she had ever let in. Or let see how powerful her energy could become under the right circumstances.

With a roar, Mack's composure broke. He pulled back, almost completely out, and slammed himself back in. It would have been painful if she hadn't already been well stretched from last night's adventures. He repeated the motion three more times before collapsing on top of Disrayan. His body enveloping hers as their energy melded completely and they became one. Better than any regular orgasm, they were cocooned in a euphoric bubble of their own making. A shimmering grey bubble surrounded their bodies.

"No matter what happens, Rye. My heart will always belong to you," Mack whispered as their combined energy receded.

She didn't bother replying, his even breathing telling her he had already gone back to sleep. Disrayan reveled in the feel of his weight on her. The warmth of his body, the familiar smell of his skin. The musk of their lovemaking hung in the air. She wished she could fall asleep with him. To continue to exist outside of reality for just a bit longer.

Instead, Disrayan rolled him onto his side, dislodging him from her orifices. She felt empty, and not just physically. Her heart ached as she watched him snuggle her abandoned pillow. For a moment, she let herself believe his whispered words. With a shake of her head, Disrayan went into her bathroom to shower off the night. She had spent enough time in La La Land.

As if to affirm her decision, Disrayan received a text from Zazzie.

"Enora's Now!"

...

Enora's condo was close to the downtown area. A beautiful little brick Tudor style with a small manicured lawn and a short drive. If Disrayan didn't need to make such frequent trips back to Ceres, she would undoubtedly have chosen to live in the quaint upscale neighborhood. Especially once Mack left. Living in the small cottage they once shared made getting over him that much harder. A small part of her had never moved, just in case he decided to come back for her.

"It's about time you got here!"

Zazzie flung the red door wide open and pulled Disrayan inside. She must have taken longer to get ready than she thought. Farrah had already arrived and appeared to be on her second glass of wine as she went over Binding ritual details with Enora.

"So, is this supposed to be a bachelorette party?"

Farrah and Enora looked up. Enora had a sad look in her eyes before she crossed the room and pulled Disrayan into a hug.

"Oh, sweetheart, I am so sorry," she sighed.

Disrayan was soon enveloped in the arms of her three best friends. All of them pouring soothing energy toward her.

"Okay, who died?"

She shrugged out of her friends' grasp. If they were this sympathetic right off the bat, then something was wrong. Even when Mack had left her, they tried joking with her first.

Farrah's eyes darkened with anger.

"I know he's my cousin, but I'll bury him deep if you choose to murder him for this."

Enora chimed in next.

"Yeah, and I'll make sure all the evidence is destroyed properly, so no one will ever find out."

"And I'll cleanse your Aura, so you won't have to carry that negative energy past the night," Zazzie said.

"Whoa, hold on. Whose murder are we planning again? Did Hendrex do something stupid?"

They all gave Disrayan an even sadder look before Zazzie handed her a shot glass full of dark brown liquor.

"Take this first."

Not exactly up for bad news at the moment, Disrayan downed the shot and signaled for her friends to get on with it.

"I was coming home from a graveyard shift," Enora began.

"All your shifts are graveyard shifts," Farrah snorted.

Enora shot her a dirty look before continuing with her tale. "I saw Mack bringing a woman home. A cute little redhead who moved in a year or so ago. Just a few houses down."

"Okay, so why am I killing him? We aren't together," Disrayan tried to play it cool but motioned for Zazzie to give her another shot.

Disrayan had smelled a hint of a woman's perfume on Mack when he came to see her last night, but she assumed it was transfer from his job. Being an analytical person, Disrayan ran the scenarios. Maybe the woman had drunk a little too much, and he was being a Good Samaritan and made sure she got home okay. With the recent murders in town, it would make sense. Then again, if she lived in this neighborhood, she could more than afford a cab home. If she had red hair, it could have been his boss, Molly.

When she rode in the van with the other Vampires, they had briefly discussed Mack helping them get a man named Shane the help he needed and how Molly was appreciative. Besides, even if he brought her home, whomever the woman was, Mack came to her last night. He'd been in her bed, and he sure as hell hadn't just been in someone else's. Disrayan would have been able to tell. At least, she thought so.

Frustrated with herself, she signaled for a third shot. Her friends huddled silently on the other side of the kitchen counter studying her. By the fourth shot, she was sure of what she believed and what she would do about it.

"Like I said, Mack and I are not together. Whatever he did or didn't do is none of my business." Her words came out a bit slurred as the alcohol hit her bloodstream.

"Yeah, that is not what we are doing. Come on, lady. We are going to go visit this heifer," Farrah said pulling Disrayan toward the door.

Inebriated beyond her limit, Disrayan didn't put up much of a fight. If she was honest with herself, no matter the situation, she was still suspicious and hurt.

"Here we go, ladies, let's at least try and be somewhat classy about this."

Enora's urgings fell on deaf ears as they made their way a few houses down and knocked on the woman's door. They waited and waited, enough time for Disrayan to regret this decision while also becoming more pissed off that the woman wasn't answering.

They were about to give up when the door swung open, and a pissed off redhead in a silk nightie glared out at them.

"Do you know what time it is? I fucking work nights."

Her red hair fell in bountiful curls around her pale freckled shoulders. This woman couldn't be further from Disrayan in looks. To make matters worse, Disrayan could feel the lingering energy of Mack and arousal coming from inside. Something else bugged her about this woman. Disrayan opened herself up more, testing the energy of the space. She quickly retreated when she sensed what the woman was. A Vampire, and yet her energy read higher than all of the Ruling Council combined.

"Sorry to bother you, wrong house."

Disrayan shrugged and tried to make a getaway, but the woman reached out and touched her shoulder. Her glare fell as recognition lit her eyes.

"You're Mack's ex-girlfriend," she said.

Disrayan sighed and turned back around.

"Yes, I am." She crossed her arms over her chest, trying to regain a tiny bit of her dignity.

"I'm Molly. It's nice to meet you. Mack is super secretive about his life, but I knew as soon as I saw you together at the club that you meant a lot to him," Molly said with a pleasant smile that showed just the slightest bit of her fangs.

"Oh, um, sorry to have bothered you," Disrayan offered lamely.

"No worries. I understand. The men that do you wrong are the ones we do the craziest things for. Just don't give Mack too hard a time when he comes crawling back. He loves you, and I can tell you still love him, too. Now, if you'll excuse me, I need to get back to sleep. I don't want to be a complete monster tonight," Molly said before slamming the door in their faces.

Disrayan stood there shocked before turning angrily to her friends who had already retreated to the sidewalk.

"So, what did she say?" Zazzie called out.

Disrayan flicked her off and stormed back to Enora's. Her buzz killed by her complete and utter embarrassment. She could only hope that Molly didn't mention a word of this to Mack. There was no way she could live that travesty down.

To make matters worse, she had more questions and suspicions now than ever. *Was Molly Aura and a Vampire?* There was no precedent for that, other than maybe, the myth of Maura. Disrayan made a mental note to dig deeper into the Archives when she went back to Ceres. If Vampires and Aura were coexisting in that way, maybe Hendrex's plan to integrate the Aura of Ceres wasn't so crazy after all. Molly could be the proof he needs, not only to win over the rest of the Ruling Council, but to save himself from Ruling Three's crazy scheme. Now more than ever, Disrayan needed to convince Mack to testify, and if possible, to bring Molly with him.

Truth

"Is magic real?"

The question caught Mack off guard. He nearly dropped the bottles of vodka he'd been putting away behind the bar. He was already distracted by his night with Rye, and what exactly that meant for them. Still, he should have known the questions would come, especially after her episode and their chat last night.

"You're a Vampire," he said plainly.

He finished putting the bottle away and turned to look at his boss, who scowled in his direction.

"Look, I know there is a lot in this world that isn't known to humans, but I know you know. Is magic real, or is it something else?"

Molly sat on the other side of the bar, looking innocently up at him with her big eyes and fiery red hair.

Mack knew she wasn't asking for no reason. Molly may not know it, but she was an Aura. A powerful one at that. The crazy part was knowing Molly's story; it made his blood boil. She was a lost one. An Aura child deemed Auraless because their energy was too weak or nonexistent. The joke was on the Aura. Molly may be a special case given her unusual turning, but who's to say there weren't other children who came into their energies late? Who wandered the world confused or unaware of their natural ability?

"Magic, sure, but it doesn't come out of thin air. Everything has an energy to it. You just have to learn to read them," he said.

"So, like a vibe you get around someone," she said.

Mack shook his head.

"Sure, we'll go with that," he said and went back to stocking the bar.

Molly seemed content with the answer, going back to updating the inventory, but then, she stopped and stared at him.

"I think I met someone who knows how to read them," she said.

"Really, where?"

"At the council meeting. One of the council members had a woman who came to read me," she said.

Mack's blood ran cold. He forced himself to play it cool. He needed more answers now. He had bailed when the Vampire Council came to visit, and now with the trafficking ring, it couldn't be a coincidence.

"Was she working for him?"

"Yes and no. She was a blood slave. I didn't even know

that was a thing. It's awful, and I wanted to do something to save her, but..."

Molly trailed off. Mack could feel the shift in her energy, going from its usual maudlin to a deep red rage. He stopped what he was doing and turned to her. Molly's eyes were closed, and her mouth moved to form numbers. After a minute, her energy calmed, and she opened her eyes. They shone with tears.

Mack placed his hand over hers and took away the last of the negative energy she held. He inhaled deeply, waiting for the energy to be absorbed and extinguished, but instead, it mixed and mingled with his own. For the first time, he noticed the bond between their energies and a surge of protectiveness went through him. The only other time something like that happened was with Disrayan. Come to think of it. He should have had a crash after absorbing the massive amount of energy Molly exuded last night. Instead, he'd been perfectly fine and completely able to keep up with Disrayan's demanding sexual escapades.

"You did what you had to do. There wasn't anything for you to do at the time. You were in just as much danger," he said.

Molly smiled up at him, her elongated canines a jarring sight. Molly may have been an Aura once, but now, she was a Vampire. Mack had to remember that. She was his mark, not his friend. He was here to observe and gather intelligence, that was it. He couldn't afford to be this close, to get so attached, but it was happening anyway. He knew it. In his heart, he already considered Molly family, like a little sister.

"I'm always in danger," she whined and toyed with a lock of her curly, red hair.

Not wanting to touch that subject, Mack decided to change the topic of conversation.

"So, did you decide what you are going to do about

Shane?"

Molly glared at Mack before a devious smile graced her lips.

"Are you going to spill about the gorgeous woman who came to see you the other night?"

Mack stilled before forcing himself to relax.

"All right, I'll stay out of your business," he laughed and went back to work.

Part of him wanted to confide in Molly. If anyone could give him insight into Disrayan's mindset, it would be her. Mack may not have left Disrayan to die, but the outcome was the same. She hated him for what he did, but loved him enough to let him back into her bed on a non-committal basis.

"Seriously, Mack. I know you are a private person, but I know a lover's quarrel when I see one. When you're ready to talk, I'm here. Besides, it would be nice to work on someone else's relationship for once."

Mack sighed and turned back to her.

"Her name is Disrayan, and I'm a stupid asshole. That's the story."

Molly laughed and patted his shoulder.

"It's okay. Even assholes can be redeemed."

Mack rolled his eyes.

"I left her at the altar."

Molly hissed in disbelief and pushed back from the bar.

"But you still love her," she said.

"I do."

"So, why did you do something so stupid?"

"I couldn't put her in danger."

"Then, why put yourself in danger if it means losing the love of your life?"

"Would you believe me if I said it was her or the fate of the world?"

"Ugh, you men and your life and death scenarios." She rolled her eyes and snagged a cherry from behind the bar. "You said it yourself. If it's meant to be, it will be."

Mack sighed. He *had* said that, but the fates were rarely in his favor. Gretchen came bounding in ready for her shift, and talk turned to the new developments with the hunt for Maura. Mack pretended to ignore their conversation, but he kept an ear out. The sooner the issue of Maura was resolved, the sooner he could get back to wooing Disrayan.

...

Tossing and turning on his bed, Hendrex tried to get some sleep. Just last week, he was complaining about having too much to do to get a decent rest. Now, with the chaos the investigation had caused, he'd been all but suspended from his duties as Ruling Four. Well, he was suspended, but even if he wasn't, he would be useless in his duties. The suspicions raised by Ruling Three made it impossible for him to continue as usual. Any work he touched would be overturned. Which didn't matter because he'd let Ruling Three get under his skin. Hendrex had lost his temper, giving Ruling Three the perfect ammunition against him. So, instead of in his office, he was here in bed. Failing to get the rest he would have killed for just a few days ago.

Hendrex rolled out of bed and slid on his robe. This forced break wouldn't be so bad if he were allowed to leave Ceres.

Hendrex eyed the display case in the corner. Most of his memorabilia was in his office, but this one case held his most precious possessions. He picked up the ball next to his dresser and tossed it in the air. Catching it with ease, Hendrex ran his fingers over the smooth white leather.

There was nothing obviously special about the ball. It had never been in a professional game, wasn't signed by a baseball great. Yet, this was his favorite because it had been a gift. Zarovia Monoceros gave it to him for his tenth birthday. The fact she had held it in her hands, chosen it specifically for him meant more than he cared to admit.

"I need to get out of here," he breathed.

It may make things worse, but Hendrex could no longer stay cooped up in the tent that had once felt like home. He went to the small wooden trunk at the foot of his bed and pulled out his human clothes. A pair of dark blue jeans and a crisp white button down. It was slightly wrinkled from misuse, but not badly enough that it wouldn't fade with wear.

Once dressed, Hendrex marched out of his tent and past the guards stationed outside. They scurried after him as he made his way down the path to the Garden Gate.

"Sir, the gate is—" one of the guards started, but Hendrex held his hand up.

"I am not a prisoner. I am not on any restricted movements. If you do not wish to accompany me in the human realm, I suggest you stay behind."

Hendrex wasn't in the mood to deal with any more of this. They wanted him away from his duties as Ruling Four, and that was exactly what he would give them. Besides, he needed answers. He needed to see for himself just how bad things were. It had been years since Hendrex had set foot outside of Ceres, and it was about time he changed that. Especially, if he planned to convince others to make the trip permanently.

The guards in front of the Gate straightened and bowed as he approached. He may be on suspension, but he was still Ruling Four and their boss. He eyed his personal detail one last time before stepping through the Gate. A blistering cold took hold of him at once, and his vision blurred as multi-colored streaks rushed past, and his stomach seized as if he was being thrown around on a roller coaster. He could barely breathe for a moment before his vision cleared and he became aware that the journey was over. He stood on the other side of the Gate facing the grey brick of the factory that provided a cover for the Sanctuary. He didn't remember traveling through the Gate being that intense.

Yet another sign things were more dire than the others wanted to believe. Some of their older population may not survive the stress of travel if the weakened state of the Gate remained. He took a deep breath; the air here was different. Heavier and more filling.

"Sir, give me a moment, and I will accompany you to your destination."

So caught up in thought, Hendrex hadn't noticed one of his guard had followed him. He turned to see the man bent over, gasping for breath. A green tinge to his skin, he looked ready to throw up. Behind the guard was a solid brick wall. No one else followed. The guard was either extremely dedicated to the job, or he too wanted to see what lay beyond the confines of Ceres.

"No need to follow me. Enjoy the day, see what you want, and I will meet you here tomorrow."

The guard righted himself immediately. Forcing himself not to appear as weak as he obviously felt.

"No, it is my duty to protect you."

Hendrex sighed. It was probably more that the guard didn't know what to do. He was new to the Security Force; they were usually kept inside the Barrier until at least their third year on duty. Guarding a member of the Ruling Council in Ceres was a rookie job. The Ruling Council had never needed protection in Ceres, and rarely, if ever, left Ceres to justify more seasoned security. It was likely this was his first time outside of Ceres for more than a few seconds.

"Fine, but out here, you are not my protection. We are friends. You may address me as Dre while on this side of the Gate. What shall I call you?"

The guard looked stunned. It was an honor to be on familiar terms with one of the Ruling Council. He quickly shook off his shock.

"My name is Icarus," he said.

Hendrex shook his head.

"That won't do. It's too strange for the human world. We don't want to draw unnecessary attention. Have you been given a covert name yet?"

"Not yet, sir. I graduated from academy a week before the incident."

"It's Dre, and I will call you Russ. Does that sound like something you can remember?"

"Yes, sir. I mean, Dre."

The guard smiled a nervous smile. He had to be in his early twenties, and yet he acted as if he was barely more than a teen. Hendrex didn't feel up to babysitting, but what other choice did he have?

"How old are you?"

"Twenty-one," Russ answered.

"Good, the first thing we are going to find out is how well you hold your liquor and your tongue."

Hendrex didn't wait for Russ to answer before heading off toward downtown. It was more than a few blocks walk, but he didn't mind. It was better than being trapped in his tent. Besides, where they were going, it was better they both be exhausted. In a tired state, their energy would be less noticeable by the unsavory they would encounter at their destination. It was time to visit his brother. Disrayan may not have been able to get through to Maclovis, but a personal visit from Ruling Four could not be ignored. Even if he was your twin.

...

"Fuck me," Mack cursed as soon as the door to the club opened.

Thankfully, the club had just opened and wasn't at the height of its occupancy. The bouncer, no doubt, had been confused when confronted with the spitting image of Mack and let Hendrex right through. His brother spotted him immediately and made a beeline for the bar.

"Something wrong?" Gretchen asked.

She fidgeted with her signature scarf. Most of the patrons thought it was just a fashion choice for the general manager, but Mack knew the truth. It hid the scars that even Vampirism hadn't been able to heal. Mack struggled to find the right words to describe how he felt. Even though he knew he could lie to Gretchen and she would be none the wiser, he trusted her. Counted her as a friend. It didn't matter. She followed his gaze, and her eyes widened as she saw Hendrex crossing the dance floor. A Magelor Security Force Officer at his back.

Mack shook his head. The man hadn't even changed from his white tunic before coming here. That would need to be rectified ASAP. Things must be dire if Hendrex had come himself, and with such an inexperienced guard.

"You have a twin," Gretchen gasped.

Hendrex walked right up to Gretchen and smiled.

"Yes, my name is Dre, and this is my friend Russ."

Gretchen smiled back and nodded.

"Nice to meet you, Dre."

"Gretch, can you cover the bar for a minute?"

She raised an eyebrow at Mack before rounding the bar to take his place. He moved to leave, but Gretchen grabbed his arm. She leaned in close to ensure that only he could hear. It was still early, but there were a few Vampires already at the club for the night.

"I don't know what's going on, but I'm here if you need me. Don't be too long, or I'll send the cavalry," she said.

Mack smiled and hugged her briefly. Touched she would worry about him that way.

"No need. Even if I take a little long. My brother means no harm," Mack assured her before leaving the bar and dragging Hendrex out the door.

Normally, he would take Hendrex out back, but they would need more privacy if things got loud between them. Mack held no ill will toward his brother, but the same couldn't be said for Hendrex. Mack's decision to leave had done more than ruin his relationship with Rye. It had cost him the companionship of his twin as well. Once seated at the dive bar around the corner from the club, Hendrex didn't waste any time getting to the point. Hendrex's guard sat at the bar where he could keep a watchful eye on them, but out of earshot to catch what they were saying to each other.

"I need you to testify for me," he said.

Mack sighed and ran a hand over his face.

"I can't," he replied.

"Why not? I mean, I know you hate me, but this is bigger than our disagreement," Hendrex said.

"I don't hate you. I just, I can't because I am trying to protect Ceres just as much as you are!"

"Protecting Ceres? By cozying up with the enemy? By relinquishing your responsibilities to me?"

"Maura's Men aren't the enemy!"

Mack was so frustrated he didn't realize his slip until it was too late.

"Maura? What does Maura have to do with this?"

Of course, Hendrex wouldn't miss or dismiss it. As Ruling Four, he had access to the same files Mack had been privy to.

"Maura is back. She's here in Langsmith. I'm here because I wanted to ensure she was neutralized once and for all," Mack said.

There was no point in lying to Hendrex now. He had to understand. He was here for a reason, and going back to testify would leave him open to repercussions that neither of them would be able to live with.

"Let me tell you everything before you decide your mission is more important than what I ask of you," Hendrex said.

Mack felt like a powder keg ready to blow as his brother recounted the events that transpired with the Gate and the subsequent fallout. It wasn't entirely new information, but seeing the dark shadows in his twin's eyes made him clench his fists under the table. They may not always agree, but Hendrex would always be his brother. He would always try and protect his family, and to do that, Ruling Three needed to be stopped. No way could his obvious political posturing go unchecked. Worse that his brother was in Three's crosshairs.

Hendrex smirked at him.

"I can feel your anger. Does that mean you will finally testify?"

Mack counted to ten and released the breath he'd been holding.

"I'm sorry, bro. You know, even if I told them the truth, they wouldn't believe me. Besides, given my profession is known to all, they might try and pen it on me, say that I'm working with the Vampires to kidnap those girls."

Hendrex sighed and took a sip of his beer.

"As always, more concerned with your needs. Do you want to see the downfall of Ceres so badly? Has your hatred for your own people gone that far?"

"I've done nothing but put the needs of the Aura before my own!"

Mack didn't realize he'd stood, or just how loud he got, until he noticed that most of the bar now looked at them. He sat down, and Hendrex signaled to his guard that things were okay. Hendrex knew how to get under Mack's skin.

"Really? You think abandoning the opportunity to be Ruling Four and Disrayan was anything but a selfish decision on your part?"

"You have no idea what you are talking about."

"Then, enlighten me, dear brother. Tell me what you are doing that is so selfless."

They sat for another moment glaring at each other. Both refusing to blink until the other backed down. A small bead of sweat began to form on Mack's brow. *When had his brother gotten so good at staring people down?* Maybe the job of Ruling Four had changed him more than he let on. Not willing to be the first to look away, Mack switched tactics.

"I'll talk about Disrayan when you talk about Zarovia Monoceros."

Hendrex crossed his arms over his chest. If it weren't for the shift in his energy, Mack would assume he was unfazed by the offer. Hendrex leaned back into the sticky vinyl covering of the booth. They sat in awkward silence before Mack sighed and relaxed his pose.

"Give me until Monday. I'll be off work then and have time to make arrangements if I don't make it back."

Hendrex smiled, but it didn't fully reach his eyes. Mack didn't stay for an answer. He left the bar and headed back to work. Commander Mars wasn't going to be happy about this, but it needed to be done. If not for his future with Disrayan, for the future of Ceres. There would be nothing left to save from Maura if Ruling Three got his way. Whatever his ultimate goal was, it definitely didn't bode well for the Aura.

Surprise

Waiting impatiently on the cold metal of a bus bench, Ruling Three checked the slim, black phone he used to contact Maximus for a fourth time. Either the Vampire was setting him up, or leaving him out to dry. Either way, Maximus wouldn't take this slight lying down. He stood to leave, but before he took a step away from the bench a black sedan rounded the corner.

The car slowed to a stop, and the Vampire in the passenger seat held out his hand expectantly. Ruling Three glared at the man before reaching into his pocket and providing the Vampires with Disrayan's home address that was on file. All Aura living outside of Ceres had to keep a current address on file for safety reasons.

"You'll be notified when the job is done," the Vampire said.

"Just do it quickly, and tell Maximus I don't want to be kept waiting again," Ruling Three snapped.

The rude Vampire smirked before the black-tinted window rolled back up, obscuring Ruling Three's view. The sedan

112

pulled away just as a city bus pulled up. Ruling Three hurried away before being subjected to the human masses that would come pouring from inside. He didn't want to risk being out in the open much longer.

Thankfully, only a couple of scraggly teens got off at the stop and headed in the opposite direction. Ruling Three shook his head. The Aura were too powerful to be so afraid of such rudimentary beings as humans. Unfortunately, the sheer number of them made them more of a threat than Ruling Three could discount. He pulled the phone from his pocket and dialed Maximus's number.

"What?" Maximus snapped on the other end.

"I've provided your men with the information. I trust that Disrayan will no longer be amongst us rather soon. I'd not like to be kept waiting like I was this afternoon."

Maximus laughed on the other end.

"You'll be notified when it is done. Don't call me again unless you have more cargo to trade."

The line went dead. Ruling Three gripped the phone tightly in his hand to control the anger coursing through his body. As soon as Maximus lost his use, Ruling Three would deal with him as well. He pocketed the phone.

Taking a few deep breaths to calm his nerves, he chanted, "Dispatch the dissenters, dismantle the Council, the Aura are mine to rule, and mine alone."

His energy swirled around him before settling, and with a smirk, he slipped back through the Barrier. With a whisper and a light tap, the guards he'd disabled sprung back to consciousness. They were a bit disoriented from his spell, in the perfect space to be manipulated.

"I understand times are tough, gentlemen, but please be

more alert," he chastised them.

They straightened quickly and nodded.

"Yes, Ruling Three."

They both bowed, and Ruling Three gave a nod of acknowledgment before turning on his heels and stalking toward Magelor.

Soon, he wouldn't need these deceptive tricks to get to the other side. The Magelor Security Force would be the first place purged of any dissenters, starting with that damned Farrah Andromeda and Donovan Mars. All of them would pay dearly for their disrespect. Ruling Three pasted on a smile as he strode through the outer rings of Magelor. He made a pit stop to the refugee tents, showing his face to ensure their support of him in the coming transition.

The people of Ceres were mere sheep. They craved strong leadership and were easily molded and guided by his higher intellect. So much of the spark that made his people great was destroyed by complacency. Ceres needed a good shaking up, and he was precisely the man to do it. It took longer than he wanted to get back to the Meeting House. He should have gone straight to his office, but decided to check if the Magistrate was still in the Archives, doing her best to find a loophole and ruin his plans.

Peeking his head into the Archives tent, he saw the Magistrate sitting cross-legged on the floor. Having abandoned the table, she had several archival tomes open around her. She studied each one intensely. Her lips moved subtly as she translated the old languages into the modern tongue. If she weren't so infuriating, Ruling Three would find her quite attractive. If she did find anything, it would be a miracle. Ruling Three had spent years pouring over those same tomes to ensure there was no way out of the plan he formulated. The ball had been set into motion, and despite a few minor bumps in the road, it would continue to run its course.

She looked up then, her eyes full of suspicion as she scanned the room. Her shoulder visibly relaxed when Ruling Four appeared from the Meeting House entrance to the Archives. They spoke in hushed tones. Judging by the dual frowns they wore, Ruling Three knew they hadn't figured out his plans as of yet.

That was marvelous news. The longer they stayed in the dark, the better chance his plan would succeed. The Ruling Council would be dissolved for lack of confidence, and he could step in as the sole leader of his people. Anyone who caused trouble for him, he would toss to the Vampires. Just like he planned to send the Magistrate into their hands. Ruling Three didn't need to hear anything more. He needed to finalize his plans before tomorrow. He wore a satisfied smile the entire way to his office. Victory so close he could taste it.

...

Sarah sat in the corner shaking. She didn't dare move until that man was gone. His energy radiated at a frequency that gave Sarah the creeps. He was powerful, for sure. Too powerful for Sarah to approach without significant risk to herself. Even without her heightened senses, she wouldn't be going near that man. Not after what she overheard. His entire conversation had chilled her to the core.

This Aura was in league with Vampires and openly plotted against his own kind. Primarily, a woman named Disrayan. The name sounded familiar, so Sarah forced herself to move away from the Gate. Finding safety in an alley a little farther away, she shifted to human form. Her notepad and pen tucked away behind a loose brick in the wall of the building. She quickly sketched the man's face and what he said before flipping back a few pages. She almost gave up on her search when she landed on the page showing a round-faced woman with chin-length braids.

That was her. The all-business looking woman who frequently traveled through the Gate. She'd been on the list of people to approach. Now, she wasn't so sure. If she was being stalked by Vampires, it wasn't safe for Sarah to reveal her identity to her. Her gut twisted at the thought of not doing anything to warn her, though.

Sarah had seen the woman go through the Gate earlier, but it would be hours before she reemerged. She peeked around the corner. There hadn't been much travel between realms since the Gate closed. Finding another person to approach could wait until later. For now, she would head back to camp and report in to Tyr. This powerful of a man had to be important to the Aura, and if he plotted against them with the Vampires, there was no telling the repercussions for the supernatural community of Langsmith. Sarah had been forced out of her home once before. No way would she stand idly by if someone tried to force her from another.

...

Disrayan wiped the sweat from her brow. The trip between the human world and Ceres was wreaking havoc on her body. She rested her tote on the ground until she regained enough strength to lug it to her car. Yet another dire sign that her homeland was on the brink of massive change. Ceres would soon be unrecognizable. With the infighting of the Ruling Council and the looming concern over the strength and viability of the Barrier, people were getting restless. Everyone was on edge. Waiting, praying, and hoping that when the other shoe dropped, it wouldn't mean the demise of everything they had ever known.

She glanced around to see if anyone else dared to make the trip recently. She found no evidence that anyone had. Yet, she still felt as if she were being watched. Finally, she found the source of her paranoia. A pair of yellow cat eyes stared out at her from a darkened corner. A shiver ran down her spine, and she lowered her gaze out of respect. No use in tempting the fates by angering the beasts of the gods. At least, she could take some comfort in the fact that they were watching. With any luck, they would intervene in a way that didn't mean the extinction of the Aura.

The cat came closer and rubbed itself along her legs before taking off down the alley toward the parking lot. The cat's tail swished back and forth as if it were beckoning Disrayan to follow. She hefted the large tote onto her shoulder. The weight of the precious tomes inside heavier than their physical measurements. She'd been successful in her lobbying to remove the sacred tomes from the Archives and out into the human world.

Disrayan was a masterful debater, but that didn't mean succeeding in her request had been a given. The tomes never left the Sanctuary. Had never been exposed to direct UV light. Her tote was imbued with many protection spells and enchantments to ensure their safe journey into enemy territory. Disrayan quickly made her way to her car, but stopped short when she saw who leaned against the driver's side door. Maybe the gods had been giving her a sign. A sign of danger ahead in the form of the last man she'd expect or even want in her presence. Arms crossed over his broad chest and a grim countenance; Mack looked up at her.

"We need to talk," he said brusquely.

Disrayan rolled her eyes and heaved the bag higher onto her shoulder.

"Get out of the way, Maclovis," she hissed.

She pulled out her key and unlocked the doors. Disrayan did her best not to notice the heat of his body, or the delicious smell of his cologne that wafted from his direction. Mentally, she was steel against his lustful arrows, but physically, not at all. Her taut nipples chaffed under the lace cups of her bra and silk blouse. Her car shifted as he lifted his weight from it. Before she could stop him, he slid the strap of the tote from her shoulder.

"What the hell is in here? Bricks?"

He grimaced before hefting it unceremoniously into the back seat of her car.

"Hey! Be careful with that," Disrayan protested, but it was too late.

The tote flipped over and the tomes inside fell onto the backseat and the floor of her car. Mack stood gawking at the contents while Disrayan pushed him away to quickly return them to safety and make sure no damage had been done. Inside Ceres they were well cared for and protected, but in the human world, they were just well-preserved antique parchment. No telling what sort of damage could be wrought once exposed to the elements. That alone was reason enough to confirm the dire situation they were facing.

"See, this is your problem! You never take care of what's important. You manhandle and use until there is nothing left but destruction and chaos," Disrayan snapped before closing the car door.

The tomes were now safely tucked away, so she faced off with her ex-lover. The shock of earlier had apparently wore off, and now he was back to glaring at her. That pissed Disrayan off to no end. How dare he be angry with her? She wasn't the one who ended things in the middle of their courtship. She wasn't the one who left everyone she held dear. She wasn't the one, once again, running from responsibility by disobeying a direct summons from the Ruling Council. Endangering the Secret of Ceres by cozying up to Vampires.

"You have no idea what my problem is," he said.

"Then tell me! What the hell is your problem?" Disrayan sneered.

He pulled her into his arms and pressed his lips to hers. His tongue danced along the seam of her lips as she stood stiffly in his arms. If he thought kissing her would make her more pliant to his plea, he was wrong. Even as her body screamed with the need to surrender, her brain remained in control. She pushed him away from her and spat on the ground for good measure.

They stood for several minutes glaring at each other. So many words unspoken between them, and yet the silence was just as heartbreaking. Mack broke first. With a shake of his head, he turned to walk away, muttering something under his breath that she couldn't quite catch. He took a few steps before turning back, a hard look on his face.

"I shouldn't have bothered you. Be safe out there, Rye," Maclovis said before storming away.

Disrayan forced herself to turn away and not watch him walk away, again. He was always walking away from her. She just hoped this time it was for good. She got in her car and slammed the door shut, shaking the metal frame with her anger.

What the hell had that been about?

If she could hate him any more in that moment, she would have. At one point in their lives, he'd been able to bring out the best in her, to smooth her rough edges, caress away her fears. Now, he had the opposite effect on her. Her heart raced with rage, her mind with paranoid thoughts. Disrayan couldn't believe she once imagined a life with this man, thought she knew everything about him. How could she have been so devastatingly wrong?

...

Mack ducked into the nearest alleyway and leaned against the brick wall of the building. His hands shook with anger, not at Disrayan, but with himself. He shouldn't have approached her like that. He knew the moment he saw her he'd screwed up big time. Still, the feel of her in his arms, even tense with anger, was better than nothing at all. Disgusted, Mack threw his head back. It cracked against the brick behind it, and he instantly regretted that lapse in judgment. Then again, the stinging sensation at the back of his skull was the perfect reminder of the pain he would no doubt inflict on his people if he failed in his mission.

He thought seeing Disrayan, talking to her, would help him pass the time. It hadn't. It only made things worse. He'd brought Shane back from rehab. Seen firsthand from him what ravages love could have on a man. Yet, here he was falling into the same trap. When he first met Shane, Mack never thought he would understand why Shane clung to Molly like he had. Now he knew, and Mack prayed he would have a better chance of righting his wrongs and winning Disrayan back.

A soft mewling broke into his thoughts. Mack looked around for the source. He became aware of the shifter's energy well before his eyes adjusted in the dim light. The black cat wound through his parted legs, rubbing against his ankles. Mack quickly pushed away from the wall and put his hands to his face, just in time to catch the massive sneeze that tickled his nose.

"Damn shifter!"

The cat stopped rubbing against him and moved farther into the darkness before reappearing as a small woman, not even a woman, but a teenager. Her face was round and child-like. She wore the simple shift dress common among shifters that preferred their animal form or adolescents still adjusting to their ability.

"Shh! You are not supposed to know what I am," she whispered.

"Well, you know what I am, so we're even. Get outta here." Mack tried to get rid of the child before he started to sneeze again.

She may be in human form, but the cat lady still had plenty of hair attached to her cotton dress.

"I have information for you," she pressed, coming closer.

Mack put out his hand to stop her. Any closer, and he'd soon be breaking out in hives.

"You can tell me from there," he said.

"If you are familiar with my people, you know we trade in information. If I give you information, I expect information in kind," she said.

"Look, I don't have time to beat around the bush. Tell me what you want, and I'll decide if it's worth whatever you know," he said.

Mack would have to talk to Tyr about his choice in spies. Then again, their secret group was just that, a secret. The girl was probably acting on orders previously given, that would explain how Tyr knew so much about the Gate situation.

"I think you will want to know what I do. Your mate's life may depend on it," the cat lady said.

Mack's blood ran cold as he remembered his vision of Rye slipping into the void.

"Disrayan is in trouble?"

He didn't bother correcting the shifter about Disrayan's status in his life. She wasn't wrong. Disrayan was his mate. He just needed time to figure out how that would look in the coming future.

"I will tell you all I know of the matter as soon as you tell me. Are Maura's Men still under her influence?"

Mack sighed. He hadn't been aware Maura was even on their radar, but it made sense that the eternal watchers would know. Shifters used their animal forms to gain access to many places and people. It was how they kept one step ahead of the rest of the world while maintaining their secret. The Aura could learn from them in that regard.

"I can't say for sure, but in my opinion, they want her gone as much as the rest of us. I wasn't aware shifters were aware of Maura as a threat," Mack said.

"I can share our concerns for another piece of information, but I'm sure you wouldn't agree. Besides, you want information on your mate," she said.

"Depends. What else would you want to know?"

"How a shifter may cross the Barrier your people have set."

Mack glared at the girl and shook his head.

"Yeah, you're right, I'm not willing to share that."

She smiled softly before nodding in acknowledgment.

"Stay close to your mate, Aura. She is on a dangerous path," she said.

The girl shifted back into her cat form and took off.

Mack shook his head. He should have known not to expect a direct answer from her. Shifters loved to play mind games. He stepped out of the alley and peered down the street to where Disrayan's car still sat. She was fussing with her seatbelt and talking to herself. Mack smirked knowing he still had some effect on her. He was about to march over and give apologizing another try when he noticed the other person waiting in a car farther down the block. Inside the vehicle, the person shifted in their seat as if they had been waiting for some time, their head turned in the direction of the factory. To the average person, it would appear that they were innocently waiting for someone. With the news he'd just heard from the cat shifter, Mack wasn't taking any chances. He decided to take a lap to check it out. The shifter making him more paranoid than usual.

"Shit," Mack cursed as he rounded the block.

The car pulled off, and he barely made it around the corner in time. There was a second person in the car. The new silhouette seemed familiar, but Mack couldn't quite place why. His body began to tingle, the slow heat of a vision creeping through his veins. He closed his eyes and took a deep breath as the images formed in his mind's eye. The same flashes of fleeing Aura, the whirling darkness hounding their heels, and Disrayan's panicked face as she succumbed to the void. Mack forced his eyes to open, shaking his body to rid himself of the gnawing in his gut. He prayed his vision wouldn't come true. That it was a manifestation of stress, but he knew the truth. The shifter's warning was clear—Disrayan was in great peril, and there may be nothing Mack could do to save her.

<h1 style="text-align:center">Captured</h1>

Mack made it in time to see the rogue Vampire tossing Disrayan's limp form into the back of his black sedan. His vision clouded in a haze of red, and before he knew it, he was crouched on the hood of the car growling like a rabid animal. His dark energy unleashed, creating a vortex of death around him. Like a black hole, it warped the gravity around him. The metal of the car crunched and crumbled under the force of his attack. If it were possible, the Vampire paled, and the car lurched forward, throwing Mack onto the ground. The force of the impact with the cold concrete broke his rage induced stupor.

The tires squealed as the sedan disappeared around the corner. Lightning fast, Mack was back behind the wheel giving chase. He memorized the license plate in case he couldn't keep up with the speeding car.

He dialed the only people he trusted to help in this situation and prayed they weren't too far away.

"Shane, I need you to trace a license plate for me."

"Is everything all right?" the Vampire asked.

"No, they've taken her."

"What? Taken who? Molly?" Mack could hear the ice sliding into his friend's voice at the thought of anyone touching his mate.

"No, not Molly, my..." Mack hesitated, unsure of how to describe his relationship to Disrayan, but in the sense of urgency decided to go with the truth.

"My mate, Shane. Rogue Vamps have stolen my mate."

"Number?" Shane said.

Mack rattled off the plate number, and in an instant, Shane cursed.

"The man who stole your woman wasn't rogue."

"What?"

"The car is a rental. I hacked the company, and that plate is registered to a shell company of the Vampire Council. I'm sorry, but I won't be able to trace it."

Mack's blood ran cold.

"However, there is only one place a car like that would be going with a human woman at this time of night. I'll notify the others. We are going to need back up."

The line went dead, and a second later, a text came through with the address. Mack didn't need it, though. Once the car hit downtown, he was forced to slow to a leisurely pace. For once, Mack was glad the carnival was running. It made it harder for the driver to do any crazy maneuvers, and easier for Mack to follow a car or two behind.

He flexed his fingers on the steering wheel, forcing himself not to grip so tight. His back began to seize up as his adrenaline rush decreased. The effects of being hit by the car catching up to him. It was that alone that kept him from getting out of his vehicle and confronting the Vampire head on. If he truly were a flunky of the Council, he wouldn't risk the exposure in the large crowd of young humans.

Then again, Mack would need to use his Aura ability to bolster his strength, and in his weakened state, there was no telling what the consequences of that would be. He had to wait. Wait until they reached their destination and he had back up. He just hoped Disrayan was okay. There was no telling what was happening inside the vehicle.

He reached out with his energy, feeling for Disrayan. His body sagged in relief when he felt her energy. It was faint and calm, meaning she was still alive and unconscious. As soon as they cleared the carnival crowds, the sedan picked up speed and forced Mack to hang back, so as not to be seen tailing them. They drove out of the city away from the downtown address Shane had sent. Almost as soon as he thought about calling Shane back, Mack's phone buzzed again.

Since the sedan was now headed in the direction of Xander, Claude and Shane's home, they could catch up to the sedan as well. The sedan drove farther into the woods, almost to shifter territory. Mack tried not to think about the run-down house in the woods where he and the others had rescued a group of human women from Vampire traffickers, yet the similarities were too much.

He turned the heat on in the car, even as he broke out in a sweat. His body was sending all sorts of mixed signals. He wasn't sure he would make it to save Disrayan. He needed medical attention for the injuries sustained fighting Rye's attackers, but that would have to wait until he saved her. Made sure she was okay. He felt slightly better about his situation when he recognized the black SUV that pulled up right behind him. He acknowledged that his friends were there with a quick wave out the window.

If he made it out of this alive, he would owe the men big time. If someone had told Mack a few years ago that he would be on such friendly terms with Maura's Men, he would have laughed in their face. Now, he couldn't be prouder to count Xander, Claude, and Shane amongst his very small list of friends.

...

Brody stood in the doorway, a smug smile on his face as he gave Renata the once over. She resisted the urge to cross her arms over her chest to cover her cleavage from the man's lecherous stare. In different circumstances, Renata may have found Brody attractive. He wasn't bad looking, and she had seen how charming he could be to other people.

Despite his undeniable attraction to her, he seemed to take particular delight in tormenting her.

"What do you want, Brody?"

He smirked and moved closer.

"Just to let you know your days as favorite are numbered," he said before brushing a finger across her collarbone.

Renata flinched and moved away. "You lie."

She had only just become the master's favorite. It had taken a full month of pandering to the creepy old man to gain that status. It had taken Emilia even longer than that. A chill went up her spine as she thought of Emilia's fate.

She now served as a blood slave to Maximus's most trusted guards. They weren't allowed to penetrate her with anything other than their fangs, but that didn't mean Emilia hadn't been forced to endure other forms of touching. Renata didn't know if she would be able to keep her calm under those conditions.

"The boss has a new, more powerful pet on the way. I've

already put my claim in to have you service me and me alone."

Renata scowled. She'd kill him before she allowed that to happen. Emilia's spirit broke long before Renata came into the picture. The woman didn't complain about any of it. Emilia wandered their gilded cage like a ghost of a person. A wild animal kept too long in captivity to be aware of the bars that surrounded them. She didn't have hope of escape, no hope of a better life. Renata wouldn't let her spirit be broken so easily.

Brody reached for her again, but a commotion above stopped him in his tracks. He frowned before leaving her alone in her room once more. Renata gawked after him. What he said couldn't possibly be true. She left her room to find Emilia. They weren't on friendly terms, but the woman still answered whatever questions Renata had about their situation.

"Emilia, have you been taken to any new auctions?"

The woman looked up from her book and shook her head.

"No, the master never keeps more than two of us at a time. It's too risky, even for someone as powerful as Maximus."

"Risky? Risky, how?"

Emilia glared at Renata before putting her book down.

"When there are more of us, we can share our energy. Use it to boost our abilities beyond what the elixir they have can control. At full strength, we could overpower a Vampire, even a pure blood like Maximus. It's happened before, which is why he keeps us weakened and separate as much as possible when not safely down here."

Intrigued, Renata sat on the chair next to Emilia. "Have you tried before?"

Emilia got a shadowed look on her face before shaking her head.

"No, never. I just heard about it from the one before me. She wasn't as powerful as I was, and she wanted me to try. I..." Emilia stopped, her eyes glazing over and moving rapidly as she remembered whatever happened.

Suddenly, Emilia slammed her book shut and stood.

"I'm quite tired. You should rest, too."

"Emilia," Renata pressed, but she was already climbing into bed.

"Leave it be, Renata. There are worse fates to be had than this. Our time will come soon. Be patient, and don't ruin what little good we have." Emilia pulled the covers over her head, signaling that she was no longer willing to speak with Renata.

With a heavy sigh, Renata stood and marched from Emilia's room. Emilia's words raced through her head.

"Our time will come soon."

What the hell did that mean? What was Emilia hiding? Was there really nothing to worry about or was Emilia so broken that she genuinely saw no better life at this point?

Renata made her way to the only window in her and Emilia's living quarters. A tiny rectangle that couldn't be opened and only provided a sliver of a view to the grass above. She took a cautious look around before gathering her energy and emitting pulsing waves of distress. She could only manage two or three a week, but it was her only hope. A small act of rebellion she hoped would alert others that there was danger.

She was too weak to do it more frequently. She always had to wait until the elixir was almost out of her system. They fed it to her daily, except for the days Maximus chose to feed. He liked to feed with their energy fully available. She was strapped to a chair, and he would make a perfect slit at her wrist. Her blood would drip in tiny rivulets into his golden goblet. At least, he didn't like to drink directly from the source. Just the thought of fangs at her throat made Renata shiver.

After the third and final flare of her energy, Renata returned to her room to rest. Maximus would call on her soon.

...

Disrayan lay perfectly still, controlling her breath to maintain the farce that she was still unconscious. Once again, thankful for her training as a Security Force Officer. Having learned to slow her heart rate in even the most stressful situations. It was a key skill when your biggest threat were Vampires who had such strong hearing. Disrayan's head ached, and her tongue felt like sandpaper against the roof of her mouth. She wasn't sure what they had given her while she was unconscious, but she could feel that she wasn't able to access her energy as she normally could.

Even reaching out to try and disable the vehicle or manipulate the locks hadn't worked. She'd planned to make her escape when they were still downtown. Surrounded by humans who would shield her and help her escape. Now, she had to rely on herself. The darkness seemed endless outside of the tinted windows. Not even the moon's glow penetrated the pitch black of the back seat.

"You should have tossed her in the trunk," a voice said.

"Yeah, well, you could have helped out with the male back there," another voice snarled.

The first man laughed, and she heard the whoosh of a lighter before the pungent smell of flavored tobacco hit her nose. She nearly gagged on the thick cherry scent and gave herself away. Instead, she focused on the flame. She could still feel it as he lit whatever he used to get his fix. Her years spent mastering fire energy served her well. Even in her weakened state, she was able to reach the flame energy and force it to grow and expand. She heard her captor's sharp intake of breath before the screaming started.

"Fuck! Fuck!"

"Put it out, man! Put. It. OUT!"

The car began to swerve, and Disrayan almost lost focus. She could feel the heat growing at her back as the flames caught on the fabric of her captor's clothing. The car jerked roughly to the right before stopping abruptly. Both front doors opened. Now was her time to make a move. Disrayan reached for the handle of the passenger door, but of course, it was locked. She took precious moments to fiddle with the door while her attacker was putting out his friend.

"Damn it! I got it! Go make sure the cargo isn't damaged. Maximus will kill us if she's scorched."

Disrayan had just slid out of the car. The fresh night air a welcome change to the smoky stench that filled the vehicle. She didn't wait for them to return. She stood and took off running toward the first set of lights she could make out in the distance. Sharp gravel bit into her bare feet, but she didn't care. Her feet would heal. Being kidnapped by Vampires was a fate worse than death.

Unfortunately, she was no match for Vampire speed. Thick fingers dug into her hair, yanking her back. Her scalp screamed for mercy, already damaged by the blow to the head that had knocked her out earlier.

"Not so fast," her captor growled.

Disrayan felt like weeping, knowing there was no one nearby to help her, even if she screamed. That didn't mean she would go down without a fight. She rammed her elbow into the Vampire's stomach, wincing as her funny bone met a solid wall of muscle. Her captor chuckled and began to drag her back to the car. She thrashed violently until he let go of her hair and gripped her by the waist. He tossed her over his shoulder. Disrayan dug her nails into his sides and kicked her feet. She managed to get her heel to his nose a few times before he dropped her. She started crawling away but was grabbed by her ankles.

"This bitch needs to learn some manners before she meets the boss."

It was the man she'd set on fire. His black suit charred and hanging in tatters from his lanky form. He flashed his long canines at her before pulling her closer. His body covered hers before she could get a good fight going. He buried his face in her neck, inhaling deep.

"I'm going to enjoy this," he hissed.

She felt the sharp points of his fangs scrape right above her jugular. She jerked, freeing her leg from under his, and she brought it up between his legs. Finding the mark, the Vampire roared and rolled off her. She noticed a smoldering pile of leaves just beyond the car's headlights. It was all she needed. She reached out with her energy and the pile ignited with a *whoosh*. As if the fates were with her, a gust of wind blew at just the right time and direction to send the flaming leaves directly at her captors. She wrapped her energy around them, creating a wind funnel. She kept the burning leaves upon the men until their clothes caught once again.

She knew she should make a run for it, but she could feel flashes of distraught energy in the distance. Warning her away while at the same time beckoning for her to come and rescue whoever was sending the signal. An overwhelming rage came over Disrayan. She latched on to that last blast of desperate energy, using it to bolster her own. She stoked the flames larger and hotter until the smell of burning flesh surrounded her. She was vaguely aware of headlights coming up behind her. If her body hadn't given out then, she would have watched until the men took their last breaths and were burned to nothing but ash. Instead, she collapsed to the ground, and the world went dark once again.

...

"What the hell? I thought you said your girl needed saving," Claude said.

Mack shot him a dirty look as he lifted Disrayan from the ground. He hadn't wanted to drain her the way he had, but seeing her standing there, arms outstretched, Mack could feel her rage and the height of the flames long before he saw her or the car she'd been taken in. He knew the men screaming in agony on the ground deserved the death she would no doubt have given them, but she didn't need that guilt on her.

Disrayan was Lady Justice incarnate. Her scales needed balance, or everything was lost. He couldn't lose Disrayan to the rage he felt coming in waves from her. She would never recover if he'd allowed her to continue on the path to destruction. So, he had no choice. He took her energy into him until she collapsed. It was the only way to save the woman he loved. Not from physical harm. He already failed in that regard, but her spirit and mental health needed protecting. She'd lost her life to flames before, he wouldn't let it happen again.

"We'll patch her up at the mansion, and you can both stay until she's well enough to go home. I know you would like to avoid human hospitals," Xander said.

"I'm not sure she would appreciate waking up in a Vampire den," Claude said.

"We live in a mansion. It's hardly a den," Shane said.

"While I agree that Disrayan may not like the idea, I can't guarantee any place is safer for her right now. They grabbed her from her home. You said yourself these men are tied to the Council. Your mini fortress is the safest place for her right now," Mack said.

Carefully, Mack placed Disrayan in the passenger side of his car.

"Shane, you ride with Mack back to the mansion and get them settled in. Claude and I will stay with these two and clean up this mess," Xander said.

Claude kneeled next to one of the men, his boot on the guy's charred hand. Mack could see the man's lips moving but couldn't make out what was being said. It was probably for the best. Xander and Claude would fill him in later. Disrayan was his priority. He nodded for Shane to get in the driver's seat. Shane hesitated, a cocktail of emotions crossing his face before he slid into the car.

"So, your mate is quite the firebrand," Shane said to break the tense silence.

"Was that a joke?"

"What? Does Claude have all domain over poor jokes?"

Mack couldn't help but chuckle.

"No, it's just nice to see you've regained your sense of humor."

"Yes, it is," Shane said.

They were about to pull off when a wolf appeared in front of them. Mack recognized the shifted immediately before it took off back into the trees. Apparently, Tyr was holding up his end of the bargain on investigating the Aura disappearances. That gave Mack a bit more confidence that they were getting closer to solving this thing. He cradled Disrayan in his arms, slowly siphoning the negative energy from her as Shane drove them both to the mansion. Disrayan would not like it when she woke up, but Mack would convince her it was for the best.

Except, by the time they pulled up to the mansion, Donovan stood out front with Farrah. Both looking pissed at not being allowed to enter the gate. Shane slowed the vehicle, and Mack could sense he was gearing up for a fight.

"They're friends," Mack reassured the on-edge vamp.

"They don't look like friends," he sighed eyeing Farrah's barely concealed weapons.

Mack carefully shifted Disrayan's weight fully onto the seat and slid from the car.

"Where is she?" Farrah demanded.

Donovan pinched the bridge of his nose, shaking his head. It was obvious he hadn't meant for Farrah to find out about any of this, at least not yet.

"She's in the car. I had to knock her out. Farrah, let me take care of her."

Farrah shook her head.

"Hell no! It's because of you she got mixed up with Vampires in the first place," she spat.

"Actually, that one's on you. We don't know how she became a target, but you're the one who called her in on the raid the first time." Mack was feeling petty at the moment.

He honestly just wanted Disrayan safely inside the gates of the Maura's Men compound, not to argue with his cousin about whose fault it was she was targeted in the first place. He looked to Donovan for help, but the man wisely stayed out of the fight between Mack and his future wife.

"This is the safest place for her. No one will think to look here for her."

"Really, so no one saw you and your little buddies rescue her?"

Mack frowned.

"The only two witnesses are dead."

Farrah rolled her eyes.

"Don't fucking care. She is going home with us. I will take you down if I have to."

Mack knew it wasn't an idle threat, and even with his unique energy abilities, he was no match for a very determined Farrah Andromeda. He was pretty sure no man was. Donovan was lucky she loved him, otherwise the man would have come out of their testy partnership damn near a eunuch. Reluctantly, Mack opened the car door and gently lifted Disrayan into his arms. He kissed her forehead before placing her in the back of Farrah's vehicle.

"Call me as soon as she wakes up."

Farrah's glare softened, and she smiled.

"I'll call if she wants me to," she said, and climbed into the car next to Disrayan.

Donovan clapped Mack on the back.

"I'll let you know immediately. Fill me in when you can," he said before climbing into the driver's seat and taking off.

Mack watched them disappear down the road, forgetting about Shane entirely until a low whistle cut into his self-pity.

"And I thought Cat was a handful," he chuckled.

Mack glared at the Vampire before shaking his head.

"As much as I admire them both, I don't think I would

ever want the two to meet. At least now, Xander won't have to field questions about the Aura."

"There is that. The women in the mansion are already up in arms over Maura. I don't think it wise to add to their worries at the moment."

"Speaking of, are you ready for this dinner tomorrow night? Carrie and Molly in one room?"

Shane shook his head.

"Why would I be worried?"

"You're a foolish man not to worry."

Shane looked like he was about to ask for more clarification but stopped as he noticed headlights coming up the drive. Xander and Claude were back. Shane had known the other two Vampires longer, but Mack knew feelings weren't exactly a hot topic with the trio of Vampires.

Unravel

"You have failed me." Maximus barely contained his ire.

It was so palpable that Ruling Three felt as if his phone heated a good ten degrees in his palm.

"I, what?"

"You heard me. I expect a replacement posthaste. I don't have time for your personal vendettas any longer. Deliver what you owe, or you'll be next on the auction block."

The phone clicked, signaling the end of the call. Maximus had hung up on him. Ruling Three threw his phone to the ground. It slammed into the pavement with a satisfying crunch as glass and plastic scattered across the coarse grey sidewalk. Normally, he could control his temper better than this. Would have, if anyone were around to see. It was late in the human world. The stars shining bright in the absence of the glow of the moon. His plan had been perfect. He all but set the perfect conditions for those fanged bastards to get the job done.

Despite not having the boost of a full moon, being alone,

and exhausted from the mood-altering spell he cast upon her while she studied the Archives, Disrayan had managed to fight off three trained Vampire thugs. At least, he thought Maximus would send Vampires to do the job. He'd stressed to Maximus that Disrayan wouldn't be an easy grab. That his weakling fang bangers wouldn't be able to accomplish the job. Then again, Maximus was arrogant and completely blind to the true power of the Aura. Ruling Three took a deep breath and shook out his tense limbs. It would do him no good to let his anger get the best of him now. He just needed a new plan. The Magistrate may have escaped the Vampires, but there were other ways to neutralize her as a threat.

Maclovis Andromeda may have backed out on their Binding, but Ruling Three's spies had put the two together more frequently the last few months. He smiled, immediately formulating a new plan that would rid him of the Magistrate and be an added dig to Hendrex Andromeda. No need to make her disappear suspiciously when he could discredit her for her romantic involvement with Ruling Four's own twin. The only problem was delivering an equally powerful Aura to Maximus. With his composure back in place, Ruling Three made his way back to Ceres. Unaware of the black cat slinking in the shadows behind him. The only witness to his out of character behavior. No one knew the true Ruling Three except people who were no longer alive to tell.

...

"There has been another flare," Commander Mars didn't wait for Donovan to speak.

Donovan shifted his phone to his other ear before setting the unconscious Disrayan on the bed in the guest room.

"Same place?" Donovan asked quietly after ensuring the room door was closed behind him. Farrah sprawled on the bed next to her friend. Too worried about Disrayan to pay too much attention to his call.

"Yes, this time the flare was stronger and spread across a larger area."

Donovan sighed.

"I'll check it out and report back." He hung up the phone.

Mars men weren't much for small talk, especially when it came to Security Force business. Ever since the first raid, Donovan had kept a closer eye on energy flares around the city. This particular flare had been too small to be worrisome under any other circumstances, but the fact that it appeared shortly after the raid and was semi-recurring meant it was possibly someone trying to get their attention. Was it a trap? Possibly, or it could be someone in need of their help.

Donovan grabbed the holster Farrah gave him as a pre-Binding present. He still wasn't fond of human firearms, but he'd come to appreciate their usefulness the last few weeks. It turned out, flashing the crude weapons was a much easier form of interrogation without the risk of exposing his Aura identity.

He was almost out the door when he felt Farrah enter the living room.

"Where are you going?"

He debated whether he should try to lie, but thought better of it. It was bad enough keeping the secret of his new working relationship with the Vampires and shifters. Besides, she already knew about the flare.

"The signal appeared again. I'm just going to go check it out," he said.

He waited for her to insist on coming with him, but instead, her shoulders slumped and she crossed her arms over her chest. His energy reached out to hers, registering her unease. Donovan crossed the room and pulled her into his arms. She rested her head on his shoulder and began to cry.

"I'm scared," she admitted softly.

Donovan kissed the top of her head.

"I know, baby. To be honest, I am too, but we will get to the bottom of this. We will make the world safe for the Aura."

She hugged him back, letting her energy mingle with his until both were balanced and calm. He pulled away to wipe the tears from her cheeks before pressing a kiss to her lips.

"Take care of Rye. I'll fill you in if this turns out to be anything more than some kids playing around."

She nodded before straightening her shoulders and giving him a halfhearted glare.

"Don't think you can just order me around and keep me out of the loop."

Donovan smiled and backed toward the door with his hands up in mock surrender.

"I wouldn't dare, love."

He gave her a wink before leaving. Part of him wanted to stay and continue comforting her, but duty called. He pulled out his phone and dialed Mack. He could use some back up, and he was sure Mack would want to take a look as well. The reoccurring flare was only a few miles from where Disrayan was found. It couldn't be a coincidence.

...

Tyr heard a car coming and quickly ducked behind a bush. Massive wrought iron gates opened before a convoy of black

SUVs came screaming out of the Vampire compound. Apparently, they had been alerted to the wreck down the way. He hoped Xander and his buddy were done cleaning up the mess. Tyr may be able to justify spying, but if things went south, there was no way he could get involved. That could end up messy in so many ways. Not for the first time, Tyr second guessed his involvement with the rag tag group of supernaturals.

Letting out a long howl, Tyr signaled any pack in the area to track the vehicles that just left. The scent trail of gun oil and anger was heavy in their wake. Whatever was about to go down would need witnesses. Tyr was about to head home when he heard another vehicle approaching.

A few seconds later, he picked up on Donovan's scent. Apparently, the man had done some tracking of his own. Tyr waited in the shadows, watching as Donovan crept closer to the compound. Not going directly to the front gate, of course, but around the side. Tyr's wolf raised its hackles, Donovan's intense energy felt like sharp nails racking against his hide. If he didn't shift back now, his wolf might attack out of shear self-preservation.

"Sup, man?" Tyr said, letting his presence be known.

Donovan whirled around, gun at the ready. Tyr put his hands up and smirked.

"Unless those bullets are silver, you aren't going to do much more than piss me off."

Donovan shook his head and holstered his weapon.

"What are you doing out here, shifter?" Donovan demanded.

Tyr shrugged.

"The same thing as you probably."

"I doubt it," Donovan said before pulling out a multi-tool and prepping a set of wire cutters to get to work on the chain link fence.

Tyr shook his head and stopped him before he got shocked and set off the alarms.

"Slow down, buddy. Wouldn't want the cavalry to come rolling out here. That fence is not only electrified, but alarmed. Why do you think I'm still way out here and not closer?"

Donovan cursed and took a step back from the fence. Tyr could feel him flare more of his energy, this time in a much greater quantity. A bead of sweat dripped from the man's forehead as a purple circle appeared on the fence, spreading larger and larger until there was a hole just big enough for him to crawl through. Tyr was impressed. He had never seen an Aura use their energy in that way. Hell, he had never seen an Aura use their energy at all.

Donovan crawled through the space before turning back to Tyr.

"You coming along, or what?"

Tyr smirked and shifted back into wolf form. He bounded through the gate. Excitement danced through him as he finally had confirmation of what he knew all along. It was possible for other supernatural to enter Ceres. You just needed their permission first.

...

Mack and Jaq came upon Donovan's car just before he felt the massive surge of energy come from the woods a few yards away.

"Of course, the bastard wouldn't wait," he muttered.

Taking off at a jog, they managed to find Donovan and slip

through the hole he'd made in the fence right before it closed. He wasn't too surprised to see Tyr in wolf form next to Donovan.

"What the hell took you so long?" Donovan said.

"I was in the middle of something," Mack said, being purposefully vague.

There was no way he would tell Donovan that he'd been about to get wasted until Jaq had come knocking on his door. His phone had been charging in another room, otherwise Mack would have been here sooner. Any excuse to get out of his own head was a welcome distraction from thoughts of Disrayan.

"So, we just standing here all night, or are we going to get some intel?"

Tyr had shifted back to his human form.

"Intel," Mack and Donovan said at the same time.

There was a little bit of tree line before the forest opened to a pristine lawn with zero coverage between there and the massive mansion ahead. Mack searched for any signs of Aura in the area. While he picked up on some residual energies, there was nothing to indicate that there were any Aura currently present. Nothing like the monster house where the women's fear choked the entire surrounding area.

"I know who owns this place. I hate to tell you, but if this has anything to do with the missing Aura, we are going to need more than just the three of us before we go in there. Not even that, but I'm entirely sure I don't even want to try," Tyr said.

Donovan glared at Tyr.

"You shifters always want to know everyone's business, but what good does it do if you never use that information for good? Never act with moral decency in mind?"

Tyr stiffened at Donovan's words, and while Mack agreed, he wasn't about to let this end up a bigger fight than it needed to be. Jaq, apparently, felt the same.

"Donovan, see if you can detect any energies. You know more about where the flare originated," Jaq said.

Donovan turned away from Tyr, expanding his energy. Clamping down on his own, Mack did his best to avoid siphoning the light his energy lacked. Then, he immediately pulled back, hands balled into fists. Donovan took off running toward the house.

"Shit," Jaq cursed and took off after him.

Donovan was definitely not impulsive, and Mack had to wonder what set him off. He and Tyr followed the two men. At least, Donovan didn't run for the front door. Instead, he came to a halt at the side of the house. A small window set below the grass line was barely visible. Mack felt the energy then. It was faint, but definitely there. Someone had flared from here recently. This had to be the source. Donovan knelt down and peered inside the window. His jaw set with disgust at whatever he saw there.

"We are going to need back up," he growled before getting back on his feet.

"This isn't a good idea. This house doesn't belong to just any Vampire. It belongs to one of the Vampire Council."

Mack's blood ran cold. He thought back to what Molly said about her visit with the Council and the Aura female enslaved by them. Shaking his head, Mack grabbed Donovan's arm and pulled him away from the house.

"Tyr's right. We can't just barge in there. Attacking a member of the Council will surely expose us," he tried to reason, but Donovan shook his head.

"We are already exposed. There are two Aura females being held captive down there, and they are not the only Aura presence I detected on the property," Jaq said.

"What do you mean?" Donovan asked.

"I mean, I felt the presence of someone powerful. Ruling Council powerful," Jaq replied.

"Shit," Mack cursed.

"Yeah, shit. I told you the Council couldn't be trusted. This is exactly why I advocate for Aura freedom," Jaq said.

Tyr pinched the bridge of his nose.

"Jaq, this isn't the time. I get it, but this really isn't the time. We need to get out of here before the armed ones return."

Testify

Renata felt their presence getting closer. She couldn't help the excitement that ran through her. She was finally going to be saved. She flared her energy again, knowing that they would follow it to the house. She wished she could go to the window, but there was a guard there now.

There was nothing she could do but wait. She felt them flaring, drawing in their strength to bolster her own. Then suddenly, they stopped. Right outside the window. She could feel them, so close. Seconds, then minutes ticked by, and nothing happened. Her resolve broke the moment she felt their energy recede. They were leaving her. There had only been a handful of them. Maybe they were going to get back up. Renata could only hope. So, she sat, and she waited. She waited until the sun rose, she waited until the sun set, and then reality set in. They were not coming to get her.

Anger rose in her chest, and she couldn't hold back her disappointment. Screaming at the top of her lungs, she flipped her mattress, then her desk. She smashed the tiny chair against the thick wood, splintering it into pieces. She held the thick splinter in her hand and an idea struck. She was going to get out of here, even if it was in a body bag.

The guard who ran to her room was met with a nasty surprise. She aimed directly for the heart. He hadn't been expecting it, and hadn't had time to block her thrust. Piercing the Vampire's flesh was harder than she imagined. The splinter sinking only the barest amount until she forced her entire weight into it. There was a sickening crunch as it pushed past muscle and bone before she finally hit her target.

The guard fell to the ground, and Renata refused to wait to see if he was truly dead. She leaped over his body and raced for the stairs. The guard in his haste forgot to lock the door to the stairway. She took the stairs two at a time until she reached the main floor. Carefully, she peeked around the corner, seeing the hallways dark and deserted. There was no one there to stop her. She raced forward, winding through the maze of halls, careful when passing open doors.

She knew enough from being brought up to feed to know that her best chance was to go through the kitchen. There was a back door there. She'd seen it a few times when they took her there to drain her when the master couldn't feed directly.

There was only one man in the kitchen, but he had his back to her as he waited for the microwave. The coppery scent of blood filled the air as it warmed, aiding her ability to sneak by undetected. For a split second, Renata wondered if it was her blood she smelled. She shivered thinking about it. She carefully crept toward the door, but luck wasn't on her side. The man turned; his face twisted into an angry scowl. She bolted for the door, but he was too fast. He grabbed her by the hair and yanked her back.

"Where do you think you're going?" he growled so close to her ear she could feel the scrape of his elongated canines against it.

Her earlier bravado forgotten, along with her only weapon, she closed her eyes, a weak whimper escaping her. She refused to be taken back. She refused to be used any longer. She jerked her head to the side, her head colliding with the monster's mouth. He hissed and briefly let her go to touch his now broken fang.

She lunged for the door before she was grabbed again, but this time, her hand reached out and grabbed a mug from the counter. She slammed it on the Vampire's head. Blood and ceramic went everywhere. The Vampire howled but didn't let her go. A large shard of ceramic stuck out of Renata's palm; it hurt like crazy, but she kept swatting at him. The shard cut into his pale skin as she fought to escape. She was bleeding profusely, and she could feel herself becoming weaker with each passing moment, but still she fought. She would fight until her dying breath if she had to. Tears streamed down her face, she kicked and screamed until the world began to fade. She was just about out of energy when she felt a welcome surge. Emilia.

Renata looked up to see the woman standing inside the doorway to the kitchen before she disappeared. Renata didn't have time to wonder about Emilia's help or where she had gone. Instead, Renata used the added boost to grab on to the energy of the microwave, pulling it away from its mounting and dropping it on the Vampire's head.

She hadn't been sure it would work. Her energy had never been this powerful before. The Vampire went limp, blood and gore seeping from beneath the weight of the microwave. She scrambled to her feet. Blood was everywhere, and she couldn't tell what was hers and what was his. All she knew was she needed to get as far as possible before anyone else came looking for her. She took off out the back door and headed for the line of trees.

Not even the electrified fence she encountered could get in her way. She used her energy to shield herself as she climbed over. Landing on the ground, she forced herself to keep running. She was still losing blood. They would easily be able to track her, so she needed to get as far as possible. Her adrenaline began to fade, her steps became sluggish, her body harder and harder to move. She was dying, but at least she would die on her own terms.

Renata sank to her knees. Twigs and rocks dug into her skin, but she didn't care. She let the darkness overcome her. Like a warm blanket, beckoning her into the afterlife. She could see the light; it was right there. She reached for it, but as soon as she did, a deep burning started in her belly. Licking flames danced up her arms. She screamed until she couldn't any longer. The flames engulfed her, and she felt as if she were falling into the pits of hell.

...

Disrayan felt like shit. Every inch of her body was stiff and ached like she'd been repeatedly slammed to the ground. She looked at her hands and grimaced. Her nails were caked with dirt and what looked to be dried blood. Her arms had smudges of black ash tracked along them as if she'd crawled through a fire pit.

"Oh, thank god, you are awake! I was getting ready to call Enora and Zazzie." Farrah laid right beside her.

"What happened?"

Almost as soon as she said the words, the images the previous night flooded her brain. Being grabbed from behind just as she was coming home. The car ride with the Vampires and then...

The blood and ashes all made sense now. Disrayan bolted from the bed and made it to the guest bathroom in time to expel what little contents her stomach held. Warm hands caressed her back as she heaved, but when she finally stopped, it wasn't Farrah who had held her hair and rubbed her back. It was Mack. She frowned and tried to pull herself from the floor.

Mack helped her to her feet. When she tried to take the first step on her own, she nearly fell over again. He caught her in his strong arms, concern written all over his face.

"Just take it easy, you've been through a lot."

She recoiled.

"That's for damn sure."

This time when she took a step, she was steadier on her feet, and she forced herself past him and into the living room.

"Where do you think you're going?"

"Home, what does it look like?"

"That's not a good idea right now. The ones who took you are dead, but the people who ordered it are still out there."

"Thanks for the concern, but obviously, I can handle my-self."

"You can barely walk right now."

"Well, maybe you should have left me a little energy to recover with, you succubus bastard."

Mack snorted. Disrayan knew he hated that comparison to his energy abilities, but apparently, it was no longer as sensitive a topic for him. Further reminder that she really didn't know who he was anymore. If she ever knew him at all.

"First off, if I really were a succubus, I'd have enjoyed the energy exchange much more. Second, sit down, you are about to fall over again."

Disrayan crossed her arms over her chest and glared at

him.

"You are not—" She didn't get a chance to finish as her legs buckled, and she sank onto the nearby couch.

Mack rushed over and cradled her in his arms.

"I get it, you don't like being this vulnerable, but you need to slow down. Regardless of how it happened, you need to rest in order to regain the energy you lost last night."

Disrayan wanted to fight it, but being in his arms again was too comforting. She was too weak to offer anything more than a passive resistance.

"Why do you insist on acting like you care about me?"

"What's it going to take to get you to admit that what we have is far from over?"

She studied the wall behind Mack's head, refusing to meet his gaze. For once in her life, Disrayan didn't feel like fighting him about their relationship or whatever it was. Reduced to feeling like a teenaged girl in front of her first love, her only love, a rogue tear trailed down her face.

"Rye, please. I know things aren't perfect. I know I screwed up. Now more than ever, I need you to know that I love you. I hate my life without you."

She met his gaze, and his eyes glittered with unshed tears.

"We shouldn't talk about this now."

"We'll talk now. We both know the only language we'll speak later is body language."

Disrayan snorted through her tears.

"Can't that be enough?"

"Not anymore. I don't want half of you, I want all of you. I know it's too soon to ask that you consider Binding with me, but at least, give me a second chance to prove I'm worthy."

"Third."

Mack made a face. "Third?"

"Third chance. You disappeared after the Gate reopened, didn't even call to see if things were okay."

"I was stupid. I didn't think you wanted me when I found myself alone in your bed the next morning. I hadn't given up. I just wanted to approach you at the right time, and I was wrong. So wrong. I'm sorry."

He held her closer; his energy reeked of desperation.

Disrayan placed a hand on his cheek. "I don't like it when you beg."

"Then don't make me. I apologize, I love you, let me show you that we can get back to how we were. I realize that may take time, but I'm willing to wait. I'm willing to do the work."

Mack pulled away to look her in the eyes. She didn't doubt his sincerity, but that didn't mean she was going to let him off easy. Even as her heart sang with the idea of getting back with him.

"Then, you'll testify for Hendrex."

"I told you I already planned to."

"Forgive me for not automatically believing the things you say."

"Please, Rye, I know now isn't exactly the best time, but I can't let you go another minute thinking I don't care."

"I don't think that you don't care about me."

Mack raised an eyebrow at her, and she couldn't help but smirk.

"Okay, maybe a little."

"So, are you going to let me in or what?"

He sat back and crossed his arms behind his head. Switching from the groveling of before to a cocky stance. The same bravado that had attracted her to him all those years ago. Her heart yearned for Mack, her body ached for him, and her energy reached out for him like a long-lost friend. She couldn't deny him any longer. Couldn't deny the love in her heart. She may regret it later when her brain was no longer emotional mush. When she wasn't still wrecked from the attempt on her life, but for now, she would welcome him and all he had to offer.

She straightened her posture and made a show of fixing her clothes and hair. Disrayan extended her hand out to him and smiled her most polite smile.

"Hi, I'm Disrayan, and you are?"

Mack smirked before sliding off the couch and pulling her into his arms.

"Your destiny," he said, and kissed her.

Disrayan melted into him, her arms wrapping around his thick neck. A disgusted groan from the other side of the room interfered. Reluctantly, they pulled apart. Disrayan turned to see Farrah in the corner on her bean bag chair, a book in hand.

"So, like, if you guys are going to get all sappy, can you do it in the guest room because I'm trying to read over here?"

Farrah sounded annoyed, but there was smile on her friend's face. Disrayan blushed and pulled away from Mack. Suddenly, there was a loud buzzing coming from Farrah, and she cursed before pulling out her phone.

"Duty calls. If you guys, you know, wanna consummate your reunion, please pull the sheets when you're done and toss them in the wash." With that, Farrah grabbed her jacket and left.

There was an awkward moment between Mack and Disrayan, now alone in Farrah's apartment.

"I'm not sleeping with you," Disrayan blurted.

"I wasn't going to—" Mack was interrupted by the buzzing of his own phone.

He hesitated as if he wasn't sure if he should answer.

"Take the call, it might be important." Disrayan turned away from him and marched into the guest bedroom.

She hated that she felt slighted by the fact he didn't immediately follow. This was the problem in the first place. He said all the right things, but when it came to it, she was not a priority to him. She crawled back into bed and started to doze off when there was a soft knock on the door. Mack peeked his head in, a grim look on his face.

"I hate to interrupt your rest, but we both need to head to Ceres. The trial is happening right now."

Fear raced through her at the thought of leaving Farrah's apartment and traveling through the Gate. With her body already so drained, she wasn't sure how well she would handle the crossing. Mack came to her side, his presence calming as ever.

"Let's get you cleaned up first. They can wait a bit."

...

Hendrex sat in the crowded Meeting House, tapping his feet as he waited anxiously for the proceedings to start. This morning, he hadn't been nervous. Now, with no sign of Disrayan, he was scared shitless. *Where the hell was she?* Disrayan would never be late to this. It wasn't just the lack of Disrayan that had Hendrex on edge, either. Mack, Donovan, Farrah, none of them were in attendance. A chill traveled up his spine as he eyed Ruling Three where he sat looking like a cat in cream.

With a heavy sigh, Ruling Three stood.

"I believe this is an insult to the dignity of our Ruling System. Our own Magistrate has chosen to abandon her charge," he stated.

The crowd began to murmur.

"We cannot proceed without the Magistrate," Ruling Two interjected.

"Which is why we should replace her. She is obviously biased in favor of Ruling Four. Not only because of his ties to her closest friend, but also her relationship with Maclovis Andromeda. She can hardly be impartial, and she obviously doesn't uphold the sanctity of the position as Magistrate, or she would be here on time," Ruling Three countered.

"Agreed, her absence is troubling, but it is well known her ties to Maclovis were severed with his ties to Ceres," Ruling One said.

"They have been rekindled," Ruling Three persisted.

"I can corroborate that. I saw the two of them outside of the Gate," a Security Force Officer stepped forward.

"Well, isn't that convenient?" Ruling Two muttered more to himself, but loud enough for others to hear.

"Regardless of her personal affairs, Disrayan has always been the most reliable person I have ever known. If she isn't here now, it is for a very good reason," Hendrex spoke up.

The Ruling Council turned on Hendrex.

"Your opinion of the Magistrate is a moot point at the moment, Hendrex Andromeda. While I hate to agree with Ruling Three on this, I do not wish to drag this out any longer. We were called here today to hear your brother's testimony on your behalf. He has refused our summons and now wastes our time. As for the Magistrate, it is in dereliction of her duty not to be here. An offence we cannot let go unanswered. I hereby motion for Disrayan to be suspended of her duties," Ruling One said.

"I second, and add that we move this all along and remove Ruling Four from his position as well. He has shown that he cannot even manage his own family, let alone act in the interest of the people," Ruling Three said.

There was a collective gasp around the room. Hendrex did his best to keep his anger from exploding all over Ruling Three. He was in an impossible situation.

"Wait!"

Hendrex relaxed as he heard the familiar voice. Maclovis hadn't left him out to dry after all.

...

The crowd parted for Mack; the citizens of Ceres afraid of his dark energy. He wished it didn't still bother him, but it did. Made him feel like a teenager all over again. Not respected, but feared for something he had no control over. He pulled Disrayan behind him. She was still weak from the attack, but insisted on coming anyway. Disrayan held tightly to his hand, needing his strength just as much as he needed hers.

When they made it to the center ring of the Meeting House, she let his hand go. The emptiness inside of him returned and further darkened his mood. He fought the urge to let his energy suck the life from Ruling Three. The only thing stopping him was the knowledge that in doing so he would only make this entire situation worse.

"I apologize for my tardiness," Disrayan began.

Ruling Three held up his hand.

"Apology accepted, but it has already been determined that you are not fit to proceed with this trial. Further evidenced by your close connection with Maclovis Andromeda."

Mack couldn't restrain himself. He lunged forward but was held back by someone grabbing his arms. He was about to lash out at whoever restrained him when he realized it was Hendrex.

"Calm down, brother. You won't be of any help to any of us if you don't reign yourself in."

Mack glared at the Ruling Council before forcing himself to relax. Disrayan moved from the center of the room and settled in with the rest of the crowd. She looked calm, but Mack knew inside she was just as much a raging storm as he was.

"Maclovis Andromeda, please come forward," Ruling One said.

Hendrex let him go with a slight nudge forward. Not that he needed it. He was anxious to get closer to the Ruling Council, but not for anything good. Commander Mars came to stand beside Mack. The lack of eye contact with Mack let him know Commander Mars was only there in case he tried to do something stupid. Not to provide any support.

"Are you aware of why you have been brought before us today?" This time it was Ruling Two who spoke.

"Yes, I am here to give testimony to my participation in the investigation my brother started."

"And what exactly did that entail?"

Mack sighed.

"To be honest, I wasn't involved until more recently. It's no secret that I cut ties with my brother and the Aura. I noticed a trend of missing girls occurring in the area and chalked it up to Vampire activity. Then a girl I knew was Aura went missing, I contacted Farrah to investigate on behalf of the family. At the time, I had no idea it would tie in with a current Security Force investigation. I was only interested in helping find the girl and ease the suffering of her parents."

"Suffering that was caused by your Vampire friends," Ruling Three said.

Mack glared at the man.

"Yes, Vampires were involved with the disappearance of Daphne Orion, but not the ones I call friends. In fact, it was my friends who assisted in the rescue."

As soon as he said the words, there was a gasp around the room, and he knew he'd made a mistake. If there was one thing the Aura were afraid of more than humans finding out their secret, it was Vampires.

"So, you admit you exposed yourself to Vampires and willingly endangered the Secret of Ceres?" Ruling Three smirked.

Mack wanted to defend himself, to assure them that his friends weren't part of the larger Vampire culture, but in doing so, he would also have to admit that Maura was real. That he was working with Maura's Men, and that was a whole other can of worms. If they believed him at all.

"The existence of the Aura is not a secret in the supernatural world. With the efforts of The Resistance and the renewed interest in our people by the Vampires, it is not the Aura who are a secret. As far as Ceres is concerned, most still believe it is just rumor or a fairy tale of some long-gone place. The Secret of Ceres is safe, but it would be a grave miscalculation to assume that the Aura could ever remain a secret as long as they are living in close quarters with others in the outside world."

"So, you admit it is safer to remain in Ceres?" Ruling One interjected.

"That's not what I said at all. Staying cloistered away is part of the problem. If we were allowed to be freely ourselves in the outside world, we'd be able to better protect our citizens against outside threats."

"So, you agree there is a threat? A threat that your brother has brought upon us by this foolish investigation." Ruling Three closed in for the kill.

Mack could tell by the relaxed set of his shoulders, the haughty air to his words. Mack knew then that coming to testify had been a mistake, but it was too late now. The best he could hope for was to be able to leave and take Disrayan with him. If she would forgive him, that is.

...

Disrayan sat with the rest of the masses, but she wasn't really present. Her brain still coping with the trauma of being snatched from her home made her numb to everything around her. Sure, she was pissed about being removed from the case, but she couldn't bring herself to muster any reaction to it at the moment.

Wringing her hands in her lap, she half listened as Mack was destroyed by the Ruling Council. She couldn't fault them for their questions. Mack, admittedly, wasn't the best witness to clear Hendrex's name, but he had been their only hope. Or so, she had thought. Now, as Mack was being played by Ruling Three, his words easily twisted to fit whatever ill intentions Ruling Three had. Disrayan couldn't sit and watch the dismantling of hope before her.

Even though the Meeting Room was round, the heat and anger rolling from them made Disrayan feel as if the walls were closing in. Panic skittered through her body. Lodged in her throat, a scream of frustration she dared not emit. Abruptly, she stood and left the Meeting Room. She needed to get away before her control slipped, and she did something she could never recover from.

Once outside, Disrayan tilted her head up and inhaled deeply. The air was thicker than she remembered, the purple sky nearly invisible through the heavy fog that covered the Sanctuary. If she didn't know any better, she would think the ceiling had lowered again. She couldn't say if it was a legit feeling or just her emotions getting the better of her. She had come outside to escape the pressures within. Seeing the state of Ceres only cemented her conviction to get to the bottom of this nonsense.

Never in a million years did she think she would ever be removed from a case. Then again, nothing about this case made sense. She may not be able to do anything on the inside, but that didn't mean her research had to stop there. She couldn't be waylaid any longer. Clamping down on her emotions, Disrayan made her way to the Archives. She was still a Magistrate and could still enjoy the privileges of her job.

She skimmed the ancient tomes and chose the book of the original families. It was the only book she'd been expressly forbidden to take outside the Archives. She couldn't blame the Ruling Council. This book was the foundation of Ceresian Society. Not that she could move it if she wanted. Of all the precious tomes in the Archives, this was the only one kept under magical protection. A shimmering force field acted like the glass cases in which humans kept their important documentations. It kept conditions perfect for maintaining the old parchment and animal skin book.

Her fingers didn't even touch the pages as she turned them. The shield acted as a barrier, even to her touch. She whispered the translation of the old languages. Each family had their own at that time, and thus, each entry was written in the tongue of the original author. They may have settled on the common English tongue out of necessity, but the old languages were still taught to the children of Ceres.

Disrayan smiled at the fanciful way the ancestors chose to tell the story of their formation.

If only more of her people had access to these tales. Maybe then they would understand Ruling Four and his vision for the Aura. Ceres was never meant to be a permanent sanctuary. The Aura were inherently human, after all. The only separation was a greater aptitude for wielding energy.

In fact, most supernatural were human at their core. Something many refused to admit. Disrayan began to skim the formation of the Ruling Council. It was a story that everyone in Ceres knew by heart. It was repeated every election term to remind the people to choose wisely.

She stopped when she stumbled over a paragraph that was left out of the usual retelling. It told of Ruling Five. A man chosen to be a tie breaker among the original four families. With a renewed focus, she read each word carefully. The story detailed how the Fifth turned the people of Ceres against the Ruling Council in a bid to become the sole ruler of Ceres. He almost succeeded in his plot, but the other Ruling Council were too united among themselves. The Ruling Fifth position was turned into the less powerful position of Magistrate. The same rules and structure that allowed for Ruling Five to make his power grab were still in place. The only thing stopping someone from doing it again was trust and the continued cooperation between the Ruling Council.

Grabbing her stomach, Disrayan rushed out of the Archival tent just in time to heave her breakfast onto the paved road outside. She wasn't easily sickened, but with what she just found out, there was no telling how her body would react at any given moment. Disrayan may not have the proof she needed to accuse Ruling Three of such a heinous crime, but at least, she now knew his end goal. Ruling Three wanted to rule Ceres as his own.

Everything started to fall into place. The suspicious circumstances around the Barrier failing, Ruling Three's attacks against Ruling Four, and his insistence on her removal from Hendrex's trial. Ruling Three couldn't get away with this. Disrayan just needed to find proof, so she could expose him for the mad man he truly was.

Glass Houses

Darkness crept in from all around. His peripherals dropping to nothing as tunnel vision set in. A red hue covered what remained as he focused in on Ruling Three. Smiling at the tense masses as he tore not only Maclovis but the entire governing system of Ceres to shreds. The people were being asked to vote, not just on Hendrex maintaining his position as Ruling Four, but whether or not he would be allowed to stay in Ceres or be banished as a traitor.

The voting box was passed around the room. A tense quiet settled over everyone and everything. It was now time for the people to voice their opinion on the matter. Hendrex hoped they would see reason, but judging by the daggers he felt along his neck and back, his time on the Ruling Council was no more at the very least.

Commander Mars accepted the boxes and placed them on the table that had been brought in for this specific purpose. He opened the lid on the vote for his position. The commander announced each vote out loud.

"Out, out, out, out, out, out." It was clear that the people no longer trusted Hendrex's judgment.

Ruling Three sat back, obviously enjoying the show, barely able to contain the grin on his face. It was nearly unanimous—Hendrex was no longer Ruling Four. As pissed as he wanted to be, it was actually a tremendous weight off his shoulders. If the next box was more generous in his favor, he wouldn't be exiled and could still live amongst his people. Work on changing the minds of the people without the rules and trappings of the Ruling Council getting in the way. That was a big if, however. With so many people voting him out of the Council, Ruling Three's propaganda had surely won the majority.

Commander Mars opened the next box. It could've just been Hendrex's imagination, but he could have sworn the man took more care with opening this box. As if instead of slips of paper, there was a poisonous snake waiting inside. Hendrex now faced the make or break moment. Would he be exiled from Ceres?

"Guilty, Not guilty, guilty, guilty, guilty, not guilty."

The two piles were growing with the weight of the axe over Hendrex's head. Yet as the commander got closer to the end, it was clear that opinions were split. The last vote would decide Hendrex's fate. Commander Mars paused, taking his time to unfold the last vote. Hendrex was so laser focused in that moment he was probably the only person who saw the slight tremor in the older man's hands.

Hendrex bit his lip, his body leaning forward as if getting just one inch closer would allow him to read the parchment before Commander Mars announced to the entire of Ceres his fate. It felt like an eternity before Commander Mars spoke.

"Not guilty."

There was a collective gasp around the room, some in shock, and others in disgust. Hendrex was cleared of endangering the Secret of Ceres, but he had clearly lost the confidence of his people. The weight of it settled in his stomach like a lead stone. Suddenly, there was a pair of small delicate hands on his shoulders. He looked up to see Zarovia standing behind him, tears glistening in her brown eyes. Without thinking, he placed a kiss on her fingertips.

Her energy reached out to his, and he reached back to her. As soon as they touched, his body relaxed, his frantic mind slowed and focused on the positive. He may not be in a position of power, but that didn't mean he couldn't help his people in other ways. Today was the beginning of a new chapter.

...

Tyr gripped the leather arms of his desk chair.

"You're sure about this?"

"Of course, I'm sure. Have I ever lied to you?"

Tyr forced himself to relax. He didn't mean to question her, but it just seemed so far-fetched. Then again, many would say his pursuit of entry into the fabled Ceres was far-fetched as well.

"A powerful Aura is working with the Vampires to enslave other Aura."

"Yes, I heard him on the phone discussing an Aura woman named Disrayan. He specifically offered her to them. I saw him again meeting with Vampires just a few blocks from the Gate."

"Thank you, Sarah. I want you to move on from the Gate to Ceres. I need your help with something else."

Tyr couldn't in good conscious continue to put Sarah in such close proximity to danger. She had already exposed herself to Mack, and while Tyr trusted Mack not to expose her, that didn't mean others wouldn't eventually notice. Sarah was a skilled spy, but even the pros make mistakes every once in a while. Sarah was also the perfect age to infiltrate The Resistance and sniff out any bad actors in the organization. A special request from Jaq, and another key intelligence gathering mission. They say the best way to know a community is to know their outcasts and their rebels. They are quick to provide information about the weaknesses within an otherwise normal society.

"What is more important than finding a way into Ceres?"

"Making sure that our world remains safe in the chance that getting to Ceres is no longer an option."

Sarah eyed him for a moment. He could tell she had a million questions to ask him. He was glad when she finally just nodded.

"Sure thing. Also, you should go check in with Kirk. He's been sneaking off to one of the secluded cabins rather frequently since last night's run."

"Sarah, what did I tell you about spying on our own people?"

"I know, I know, but he's been taking supplies out there, and he smells off. I don't think he is acting against you or the pack, but he is acting suspiciously out of character."

"It's only been a day. He's probably prepping to go in seclusion for a bit. It isn't uncommon for older, unmated shifters to do so."

"He isn't that old."

"I'll look into it. In the meantime, tell Sequoia you need a few new casual outfits."

Sarah made a face.

"What's wrong with what I already have?"

"Nothing, I just don't want you to wear anything that's covered with shifter energy before going to The Resistance meetings."

Sarah perked up, just like Tyr knew she would.

"That's my new mission?"

"Yes."

She smiled and took off. Tyr waited the appropriate amount of time before getting up to close the door. He pulled out his phone and dialed Jaq.

"Hey man, I've got good news and terrible news."

...

Disrayan exited the Archives in a rush. She needed to inform the others what she had found about Ruling Three's possible motives. Unfortunately, by the time she got to the Meeting Room, people were already streaming out in droves. She missed the entire thing, and now she was in full panic mode.

What had happened? Where was Mack? How did Hendrex fair in the end?

Finally able to push inside, her shoulders sagged with relief as she saw Mack, Hendrex, and Zarovia huddled together. Zazzie had tears in her eyes, but neither Mack nor Hendrex were being dragged from Ceres by Security Force Officers. She knew Ruling Three hadn't gotten exactly what he wanted.

"There you are," Mack said and pulled her into his arms.

Her frantic energy calmed as soon as his energy melded with hers.

"So, shall we be expecting two Binding Ceremonies before the elections?" Ruling Three said, laughter dancing in his eyes.

Disrayan pulled away from Mack and faced off with the older man.

"Elections?"

"Right, if you hadn't run out on your duty as Magistrate, you would know. The position of Ruling Four will have to be refilled, and that means all of the Ruling Council is in the running to be replaced."

Panic rose in her chest. The bastard's plan was already well into motion, and with the elections, there was little Disrayan could do to stop Ruling Three. The damage to the political structure of Ceres was done. Ruling Three gave the room a smug onceover before spinning on his heel to leave, his robes fluttering dramatically in his wake. As soon as he was out the door, the tension in the room fell exponentially.

Mack placed a hand on her shoulder in solidarity. She relaxed a little under his touch. Things were far from perfect between them, but at least now, there were no outside forces keeping them apart. Mack's secret assignment was no longer a secret to her.

"So, what now?" Enora stood cradling her body with her arms. She looked ashen and shaken to her core.

Disrayan knew she was truly out of it that she hadn't noticed the others arrive. Hendrex stepped forward, finished with his conversation with Donovan and Commander Mars.

"We'll have elections. Ruling Three will no doubt already be campaigning in the next hour."

Farrah shook her head, fire dancing in her eyes. Donovan pulled her against him, keeping Farrah from doing what, to be honest, most of them wanted done. Ruling Three deserved whatever came for him. A grand karmic reckoning was bound to occur at some point. It just sucked that the stability of Ceres was put at risk due to the whim of a narcissist.

"He won't get away with this," Disrayan said.

"No, he won't, and I know just how to get the bastard."

Everyone turned at the new voice in the room. Jaquis Andromeda stood just outside of the center ring, arms crossed over his chest. He looked pissed, but at the same time, a glint of mischief lit his eyes.

"What are you doing here?" Farrah questioned her brother. He rolled his eyes.

"Like I would pass up on an opportunity for real change? I don't like Ruling Three's motives, but I got to say, this all works in my favor. With fresh, new leadership, we can finally move in the right direction. Aura living without fear of being themselves."

A few of the stragglers from the hearing lingered closer as he spoke. Their eyes lit up with interest. Jaquis Andromeda was back in Ceres. That, in itself, was an event.

"We can discuss that later, cousin. I am glad you decided to take part in society for once."

Disrayan shook her head as Hendrex faced off with Jaquis. Although both men seemed poised to break out into a fight, the tension in their bodies eased, and they both started laughing. The crowd stared on in confusion. Especially, when the two exchanged a fancy hand shake ending in a tight embrace. The only people who didn't seem shocked by the display were Mack and Donovan. Which raised even more questions. It was not a secret Donovan was not a fan of his future brother-in-law.

Enora moved to stand slightly to the side of Jaquis. Looking up at him with the pride of someone invested in his future. It brought a smile Disrayan's face. She knew there was someone in her friend's life, but she never would have guessed Enora would fall for the often immature Jaquis. The energy in the room remained uncertain, but infinitely calmer than before.

Warm arms encircled her waist, and Disrayan relaxed into Mack's embrace for a moment before pulling away. The trial was over, but that didn't mean there wasn't more to do for them both. Just nothing that would keep them from each other any longer.

"When I said a chance, I didn't mean starting over. There is no good in pretending what happened between us never happened."

Disrayan couldn't argue with that logic. Even though she was willing to move forward, that didn't mean the ache she felt when she remembered the past would just disappear.

"Fine, but promise me one thing."

"Anything," he replied.

"When this whole mess is over, and we peg Ruling Three for the conniving asshole he is, you have to do the dishes."

"Really, the dishes?"

"You really want to argue when I'm asking you to move back in with me?"

Mack smiled brightly and kissed her.

"We'll take turns. You cook, I clean, I cook, and you clean."

Disrayan shook her head before kissing him again.

"We'll work on the terms later. For now, I need you to take me home."

Mack didn't hesitate in swooping her into his arms. She giggled as he carried her out of the Meeting House. For a moment, Disrayan forgot everything but the giddy in love feeling of the moment. She couldn't even bring herself to care about the stares their antics garnered. If only this could last forever. At the very least, it could last the night. All the bad could wait until tomorrow. Disrayan wasn't ready to say that everything was settled between them, but if she had learned anything from this whole ordeal, it was that life was too short to live without love.

Epilogue

Gasping for air, Renata's body twitched and jerked. Her limbs burned with the fire of a thousand suns. Her screams almost loud enough to eclipse the million others assaulting her eardrums.

"Kill me! Just kill me! Let me die!"

A pair of hands grasped her shoulders, holding her down. Cool against the raging inferno, a deep, rumbling voice whispered softly in her ear, "I've got you. You're safe here with me."

Even hushed, his voice was nearly deafening. Renata attempted to open her eyes but couldn't make out more than shapes and colors. Brown walls, brown skin, green blankets that felt like the coarsest of sandpaper.

"Please," she begged.

Despite the pain, despite her previous situation, Renata knew she was safe with whoever helped her now. He leaned close again, pressing a cup to her lips. Thick, cold liquid sloshed in the cup as her body continued to convulse.

"Drink, this will help."

She parted her lips slightly, letting the liquid spill passed her lips and onto her tongue. The sharp metallic tang mixed with decay made her retch while at the same time her body sat up, guzzling it down.

Disgusting!

Yet, it squelched the fire inside. She could almost relax into the strong arms wrapped around her. Arms that carefully held her weak body upright so she wouldn't choke on the miracle elixir.

"Thank you," she managed hoarsely.

Her voice didn't sound at all her own. It was weak and as gravely as a two pack a day smoker. Once the cup was empty, she was placed gently back into a prone position, the coarse sheets tucked firmly around her body.

"Rest now. We can talk more when you are better."

Her caretaker left the room, and it felt like she had just lost her best friend all over again. Confused about her intense reaction to the man leaving, Renata did as she was instructed. Not that she had a choice. She felt too weak to move on her own, too exhausted to even try. Not to mention, her other senses were heightened beyond anything she could ever have imagined. And to make matters worse, Renata had absolutely no memory of how she'd gotten to wherever she was. Her only memory was of running, from who or what she didn't know.

Vampires.

About the Author

Stella Williams is a blogger and romance author who lives in Washington state. She has a degree in Anthropology from The University of California, Santa Cruz. Stella prides herself in using her studies to create diverse worlds and characters for her novels. You can find more about Stella on her website

www.serpentinecreative.com.

Keep up to date with Stella Williams and her latest projects.

http://facebook.com/stellawilliamsauthor

http://instagram.com/StellaLove4Life

http://twitter.com/StellaLove4Life

http://youtube.com/serpentincecreative

<u>**Join Our Mailing List**</u>

https://mailchi.mp/2637cc1d4d12/getcreative

Stella's Catalogue

Maura's Men Trilogy

Xander's Claim

Claude's Conquest

Shane's Redemption

Langsmith Shifters

Coy Wolf

A Night Divine

Secret of Ceres

Ferocious

Dauntless